# Aubrey
## and the
# TERRIBLE
# LADYBIRDS

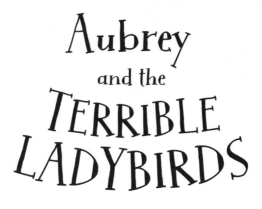

**Horatio Clare** grew up talking to animals. He started with dogs, cats, sheep and cuckoos. He now talks to Little Owls every night! (It is not difficult. You go where they are, wait until they hoot, and hoot back.) Horatio has written several books for adults. His first book for children was *Aubrey and the Terrible Yoot* and it was more fun to create than anything he has made before. Horatio thinks all children should read, write and talk to animals, and he is keen to help them do that whenever he can.

# Aubrey
## and the
# TERRIBLE
# LADYBIRDS

## HORATIO CLARE

### ILLUSTRATED BY
### JANE MATTHEWS

Firefly

First published in 2017 by Firefly Press
25 Gabalfa Road, Llandaff North,
Cardiff, CF14 2JJ
www.fireflypress.co.uk

A CIP catalogue record of this book
is available from the British Library.

Print ISBN 9781910080504
epub ISBN 9781910080511

*This book has been published with the support
of the Welsh Books Council.*

Design by: Claire Brisley
Printed by: Pulsio Sarl

For Aubrey, Robin and Rebecca,
with love to the moon and stars
(and back again).

# Aubrey and the Terrible Ladybirds

**Starring:**

**Aubrey** – Our hero. Works hard at school, sometimes. Adores but does not always listen to his parents. Believes in Living Life to the Full. He is able to talk to animals, and to understand what  they say. Animals know him as AUBREY RAMBUNCTIOUS WOLF.

**Jim** – Aubrey's father, an English teacher at Aubrey's school. Loves his family, books and walking, and sometimes gets into trouble.

**The Ladybirdz Family**
– Rosso, Rodina, Zenya,
Bronko and Pikola, a
travelling family. They love
each other, and aphids.

**Suzanne** – Aubrey's mother, a
nurse, a runner. Loves Aubrey
and Jim and sometimes has
to rescue them, which she is
very good at.

**Ariadne** – An
extremely large house
spider. Loves flies and
travel, hates baths.

**Hirundo** – A swallow, a
traveller, a talker. Loves
lady swallows, hates bat
hawks and traffic.

**Mr Ferraby** – A retired gentleman, a good neighbour, a maker of mobiles, observer of animals and birds, friend of Aubrey and his family.

**Mrs Ferraby** – Retraining as a psychologist since she retired. Loves hard work and Mr Ferraby, whose ideas about animals and birds she thinks are batty.

**The Unfriendly Ladybird**, also known as the **Historian Ladybird** – A native of Rushing Wood and guardian of the Ferrabys' garden. Loves aphids, suspicious of strangers.

**Aloysius Wolf von Wolf** – An eccentric German wolf spider, efficient, loves time-travel.

**The Terrible Cockerel** – An Italian cockerel. Eats whatever he can, hates the British.

**Bernardo** – An Italian honey bee. Loves nectar, vines and roses, conversation and Ariadne.

**Eric** – A French worm. Loves soil, hates fertiliser, hates birds, friend of Ariadne, suspicious of the English.

**Pascale** – A schoolgirl, clever, passionate and friend to animals and insects. Hates pesticides and prejudice.

 **Hoppy** – A grey squirrel, a famous character in Rushing Wood. Loves pranks, action and teasing; hates buzzards and goshawks.

Other parts are played by members of the Great Family of the Creatures of Rushing Wood.

# CHAPTER 1

# The Newcomers, and Trouble on Woodside Terrace

One bright morning of wind and surging waves, a white ship came into port. All night the waves had been big bucking thumpers which had made the ship sway and roll. It had been a rough crossing for the family who now stood on the top deck. Rodina, the mother, felt seasick. Pikola, the youngest child, had been seasick. The two older children were tired. Their father, Rosso, tried to cheer everyone up.

'Look!' said Rosso in his jolly way. 'Look – a new country! A new adventure!'

Rosso was a bulky, happy father. 'Isn't this exciting?' he cried. 'Hello, new world!'

He waved at a man on the dock who was hooking the ship's ropes over bollards. The man did not see him or hear him.

Rosso's family stared down at the new world. They saw metal cargo containers and they saw cranes. They saw cars, roads, a cold sky and a freezing grey sea.

'It's disgustick!' said Pikola. Disgustick was her favourite word at the moment. 'I don't want to go on holiday here.'

'Ah-ha!' said her father. 'It's time I told you about the next part of our Great Adventure. We're not just on holiday. We're coming here to live. We're going to start a new life in this new world and it will be wonderful!'

The second oldest child was called Bronko. Because his big sister Zenya often took charge of him, or tried to, and because his little sister Pikola was very good at getting what she wanted, Bronko would shout and roar when he wanted to make a point. 'OH NO! I HATE EVERYTHING!' he howled.

Pikola burst into tears. 'I don't want to live in a disgustick place!' she wailed. 'I want to go home!'

'Calm down please, children,' said their mother, Rodina. 'This is a famous country. It is one of the most beautiful places in the world and one of the kindest places in the world. Everyone knows it is a safe and special land. We will meet lots of friends. We will make our home here – a happy home, I promise you.'

She gathered her children around her. 'You've done so well,' she told them. 'Dad is proud of you and I am proud of you. So keep your spirits up for the next bit – it's not far now, and then we can all relax, OK?'

The children saw that their parents had made up their minds. Zenya quite liked the thought of new places and new friends.

'You guys are unbelievable,' she said. 'At least it can't be worse than this.'

'It isn't worse – it's magical!' said Rosso. 'Are we ready, everybody? Ready, Rodina my love?'

'Yes we are!' said Rodina. 'We're always ready, aren't we, kids?'

'Come on then!' hollered Rosso. 'Forward, to the New World!'

Rosso opened his wing covers, took off and flew over the ship's rail. Rodina and the three children took off too. The family flew in a tight formation. They headed west, on a course for Woodside Terrace.

At Number 6 Woodside Terrace, up in his attic room, Aubrey was celebrating the start of the Easter holidays. Having built a battleship out of Lego he was now using his catapult to fire Lego bricks at it. Every time he hit it, bits of Lego blasted around the room and Aubrey cheered.

Perhaps he was adding a bit more force to his shots than necessary, and cheering a bit more loudly than he needed to – and there was a reason for this. He was trying to take his mind off the Start of the Holidays Argument which his parents, Jim and Suzanne, had been having downstairs.

Jim and Suzanne seemed to be having a lot of arguments at the moment. Sometimes they were little, about Suzanne not doing the washing up when Jim thought it was her turn, and sometimes they were larger arguments, like Suzanne saying the house was too small and they ought to move somewhere bigger, and Jim saying she was wrong. Aubrey knew they loved each other really, and he knew arguments were part of life, but he hated the dark look that came over Jim's face, and the tight look that came over Suzanne's sometimes.

The Start of the Holidays Argument was about the garden – Suzanne wanted Jim to clear it up, and Jim said he had his marking to do and no time for the garden. He said Suzanne should clear it up. Suzanne said she had done the shopping and the laundry and the clearing up inside and why didn't Jim do something for a change?

The argument had gone quiet now, but Aubrey was still making himself feel better by firing bricks at the battleship.

Downstairs, Jim was reading the newspaper. He stopped and read closely.

'The little monsters!' he cried. 'We'll have to look out for them!'

Suzanne had just put the fish pie in the oven.

'What monsters?' she asked.

'Killer Ladybirds!' Jim cried. 'It says we have to patrol the garden and if we see any, to get rid of them.'

Suzanne made a face. She was fond of animals, plants, insects and all living things except spiders. Whenever Jim got excited like this and talked about getting rid of the jackdaws which roosted on the chimney, or the mice who lived under the stairs, or the swallows nesting in the eaves, or the starlings which sat about on the roof all day whistling at the runners as they went up the lane, Suzanne argued with him.

'Why can't you just live and let live? You know Aubrey loves animals, and I do. It really annoys me when men go on about getting rid of things and shooting things.'

'You don't like spiders,' Jim returned. 'I don't like killer ladybirds. What's the difference?'

'No, I don't like spiders, but I don't go around shooting them or getting rid of them,' Suzanne said. 'Nurses believe in saving lives, not taking them away.'

'No one's talking about shooting Killer Ladybirds,' said Jim. 'But the newspaper says we have to get rid of them.'

'Stuff the newspaper,' said Suzanne.

'Stuff the Ladybirds! The Official Advice is to get rid of them,' said Jim.

'Stuff the Official Advice,' said Suzanne.

In the house next door, Number 5 Woodside Terrace, Mr and Mrs Ferraby had finished their supper.

'They can't be that bad, dear,' said Mrs Ferraby. 'They're only little insects! Newspapers exaggerate, don't they? Who are these ladybirds going to kill?'

Mr Ferraby pointed at the map in the newspaper. 'They've even invaded America, Eunice. Imagine that – America. If they can invade America they can invade anywhere. They could invade Britain like that.' Mr Ferraby snapped his fingers dramatically.

Mrs Ferraby said, 'Britain invaded America

once upon a time, didn't it?'

In his most important voice Mr Ferraby said, 'We're not talking about history, we're talking about Right Now. These ladybirds have got to be stopped. Or they will scoff all the aphids and our ladybirds won't have enough aphids to eat.'

'Do you like aphids?'

'You know I don't, Eunice. They eat my plants,' Mr Ferraby said.

On the windowsill of the Ferrabys' house, behind the plant pot, Rodina turned to her husband and their three children.

'Did you hear that? They think we are invading,' said Rodina. 'The man says we have to be stopped.'

'We must hide,' said Rosso. 'We must not be seen.'

'Are we invading, Mum?' asked Pikola, the smallest large ladybird child.

'Don't be silly,' said Rodina. 'Five of us! We couldn't invade a puddle of water. We'll get down low and keep still.'

Jim went into the garden. Mr Ferraby came out of his back door. After discussing the weather, which was lovely and warm, and their gardens, Jim asked if Mr Ferraby had heard about these Killer Ladybirds.

'I have indeed!' Mr Ferraby cried. The men agreed these creatures were a serious threat which Mrs Ferraby and Suzanne did not understand. Their wives would be no help to them: they would have to keep watch and mount patrols themselves. They were both delighted to have the other's help.

'I think we should do our first patrol right now!' Jim cried.

Mr Ferraby agreed. 'What sort of equipment will we need if we find the blighters, do you think?'

'A fly whisk or something would do it,' Jim said. 'I'll just see what I have.'

The men went back into their houses. A minute later Mr Ferraby had a rolled-up magazine and a bottle of anti-mosquito spray. Jim was armed with the spatula

Suzanne had used for the fish pie, and a wooden spoon.

They set off.

'Any sign your side?' Jim called.

'Nothing yet,' Mr Ferraby answered. 'How about you?'

'Plenty of earwigs and spiders,' Jim said, 'but no Killer Ladybirds.'

He swatted the air with his spatula, practising.

'It gets very thick at the top here,' Mr Ferraby called, panting a bit. 'Wait a minute! I think there is something up here! Yes! My goodness – there are ladybirds – big ones! But I can't get to them!'

'I'm coming!' Jim shouted, and he charged at the fence and began to struggle over it, fighting his way through a hawthorn tree. 'Ow!' he shouted. 'Oof!' he cried, as he tumbled through it into Mr Ferraby's garden.

'Do you see? Up there?' Mr Ferraby pointed into the thick bushes. 'There's a herd of them under that!'

'Charge!' shouted Jim, and he did,
plunging forward and striking wildly ahead
of him with the spoon and spatula.

'Killer coming this way!' shouted Bronko.

'Help!' screamed Pikola. 'A DISGUSTICK
MAN!'

'Come to me, children!' yelled Rosso.

'A mad brute!' yelled Zenya. 'A monster!'

'Don't panic,' said Rodina, calmly. She

was very good in an emergency. 'Follow me, children: this way, Rosso. It's only one silly man. We'll escape easily – this way.'

The little family scuttled around a mass of ivy, trundled over some rocks and nipped under a rotten branch where they stopped, hidden from Mr Ferraby and Jim.

'Are they trying to kill us, Dad?' Bronko whispered.

'Why did he chase us, Mum?' wailed Pikola.

'Hush,' said Rodina. 'He's just silly – he charged into that bush and got stuck, didn't he? We don't have to worry about either of them!'

'Your mother is right,' Rosso said. 'They're much too slow and clumsy to be dangerous. We will keep an eye out for them and we won't worry. Besides, you always have an adventure when you discover a new place!'

They could hear voices in the garden, a woman's voice they did not recognise and the voice of the man who had tried to swat them, but they could not work out what was being said. The voices were arguing.

Up in his attic Aubrey could also hear the argument, and he could hear what his parents said. These rows put a miserable feeling in the middle of his tummy.

'You silly man!' Suzanne shouted. 'What on earth do you think you're doing? Smashing about in the Ferrabys' garden with a wooden spoon. Have you lost your mind?'

'I was protecting us from these weirdo ladybirds!' Jim retorted.

'You're the weirdo,' Suzanne replied. 'Why can't you just leave the creatures in peace?'

'It's easy for you to criticise when you don't know the facts,' Jim said. 'The newspaper said that these ladybirds are dangerous!'

'Oh, rubbish. Charging around with a spoon, acting like a maniac! Those ladybirds have as much right to be here as you do.'

'Well I don't want to be here if you're going to shout at me for trying to do the right thing.'

'Good! I don't want you here if you're going to behave like a delinquent.'

'Right! Well I'm going to go to town and have my supper there.'

'Fine! You do that. And don't come back until you're ready to behave like a responsible man, and set a good example to Aubrey.'

'I set a fine example!' shouted Jim.

In the attic Aubrey wiped his eyes. They got wet again and he dabbed them with a piece of tissue paper until they stopped. He threw himself on his bed and covered his head with his pillow. He felt as though his stomach was slowly tightening in a horrible way. 'Make them stop,' he said to himself.

'Hey,' said a small tinkling voice, a beautiful, musical voice like tiny silver bells. 'Hey. Cheer up.'

Aubrey sat up. Where had that come from?

If you have come across Aubrey before, you

will know that he is an unusual boy. Like any child he can talk to animals; unlike most children he can also understand what they say. Animals are very fond of children. Children notice more of the world than adults do, and so animals talk to them often.

Pigeons are interested in what you are wearing and they comment on it: 'Nice shoes! Got any crumbs?'

Blue tits know everything. News travels between blue tits much faster than it does on the Internet.

Swallows are always telling anyone who will listen about their travels.

Cats think aloud and they are quite sarcastic, and everybody knows dogs tend to talk about food and love, love and food, walks and cats, food, love and other dogs.

When any animal talks to Aubrey he hears them in his head, the same way you are hearing these words as you read them.

'Who's there?' he said, aloud.

'I'm Ariadne,' said the voice. 'I'm over here.'

You would not have thought that Aubrey's day could get much worse. He looked over at the table where he did his homework, and there, crouched on the corner, waving one long spindly leg at him, was a gigantic house spider.

Seeing the spider gave him a fright. Then he groaned. He let his head flop back on the pillow.

# CHAPTER 2

# More Trouble

'Bad day?' Ariadne asked, gently.

Being able to talk to animals doesn't mean Aubrey likes all of them. He has little time for slugs, which are quite morose creatures, always complaining that lettuce is not as nice as cat food, and cat food is not as nice as steak – and why doesn't anyone ever leave them any steak?

As for spiders, Aubrey has never spoken to one. They give him the creeps. Nothing he knows about them suggests they are the kind of insect it would be fun to know. Lots of eyes. Eight scuttly legs. Sticky webs. Sucking the juice out of prey...

He avoided spiders and they avoided him. But having someone to talk to was better than crying into his pillow, and Ariadne had a kind voice, even a beautiful voice, if you didn't look at her.

'Yeah. My parents are having a row. I hate it when they argue.'

'Suzanne and Jim?' the spider said. 'We all like them so much! Is she going to eat him?'

'*What?*'

'Is Suzanne going to eat Jim?'

'Of course not!'

'Some spiders sometimes eat their husbands,' said Ariadne, calmly.

'*Yuk*! Why?'

'Oh, well, you don't really need a dad around if you are a spider. And if you eat him you can put him to good use. He makes you fit and strong, which is good for your eggs – so it's actually good for his children if you eat him.'

'Spiders are disgusting!' Aubrey exclaimed.

Ariadne made a small sniffing sound. She seemed to shrink a little.

'Sorry,' Aubrey said. 'I take that back.'

'I understand,' Ariadne said, quietly. 'I know I disgust you. We disgust humans and so humans kill us. Cousin Agnes got the hoover from your neighbours at Number 7. Agrippina too, my aunt, she had the slipper. It was quick. Granny Ansell was stamped on – footwear runs in the family. My mother's cousin Anthea was drowned. Mrs Ferraby next door turned the shower on her. We know how it goes. When the Great Hunger comes you will only have yourselves to blame.'

Ariadne's gently spoken words gave Aubrey a cold feeling which made him forget, for a moment, the problem of his parents.

'The Great Hunger? What's that?'

'Ah! Nothing! Forget I said it,' said Ariadne, quickly. 'Your poor parents! Humans get into such terrible twists. Loving each other and having children is so easy. Animals could teach you but you don't pay us any attention. Well, *you* do, but most

people don't.'

'What's the Great Hunger?' Aubrey
demanded, refusing to be distracted.

'Oh, lawks!' cried the spider. 'I really
shouldn't have mentioned it!'

'Tell me what it is!'

The little boy realised he was tired,
miserable, and now he sounded rude. He
moaned at himself but it sounded as though
he was whimpering at Ariadne.

'Please!' he whimpered.

'You don't want to know,' said Ariadne, quietly. 'It's rather horrible. It would make you scared.'

At that moment they both heard Suzanne's voice calling up from downstairs.

'Aubrey!' she called, 'Can you come down please? It's supper time.'

With a feeling of dread Aubrey stood up.

'I'll see you later,' he said, and he went downstairs, hoping that his parents would not be shouting at each other.

'Dad's decided to have his supper in town,' said Suzanne. She was doling out the fish pie, banging lumps of it onto two plates.

'You had a row.'

'Yes. Silly man. He'll calm down.'

'Why were you angry with him, Mum?'

Suzanne explained about the ladybirds, and Jim and Mr Ferraby making their raid on the bushes. It sounded silly to Aubrey.

When she had finished speaking, Aubrey

ate his fish pie in silence for a while. Then he said, 'Do you still love him, Mum?'

'Oh yes,' said Suzanne, 'of course I do. But loving someone doesn't mean you don't argue with them. And when you disagree about something you have to work it out, or the arguments just get worse. When people don't change their behaviour it can be very difficult, because you get bored and angry with some of the things they do, and you feel like they don't respect your feelings.'

'Does Dad respect your feelings?'

'Most of the time!' Suzanne smiled. 'And I respect his. But we disagree about some things, and that's just the way it is.'

# CHAPTER 3

# The Swallow Stone

There was a beautiful soft light in the sky when Aubrey crashed down on the bed in his attic room. It seemed to be the first of the long evenings and it was warm enough to have the window open.

He lay staring at the treetops. He was miserable. He was thinking about Jim and Suzanne. What if they could not respect each other's feelings? They did seem to be arguing a lot. Aubrey wondered if they would split up. He had friends at school whose parents had split up after they had stopped loving each other. But he had never heard of anyone splitting up because of an argument over ladybirds. Aubrey was not sure if this was a comforting thought or not.

At that moment there was a wild

twittering outside, and a fluttering of sharp wings, and a bird landed on the windowsill.

'*Phee-ew!*' said the bird. 'Made it!'

The bird was sleek, with a deep-blue back, a red patch like a small helmet on his face, and a bright white breast. He had a very slight South African accent.

'Hey, Aubrey!' the bird exclaimed, looking at him with shining dark eyes. 'Seen any of the others?'

'Any what?'

'Any other swallows! Have you seen any other swallows?'

'No.'

'YES! I WIN! I'm the First Back! Tra-laa! What a *flier* I am! I mean I am *good*. No way round it! I'm so hot I make lightning look cold.'

'Were you racing?'

'Was I racing! Yes I was – and I'm First Back – so I won! Hirundo is *THE WINNERRR!*'

'Well done you,' said the boy, beginning to

smile. 'Have you come a long way?'

'Only about six thousand miles,' Hirundo
said, coolly. 'Crossed the whole of Africa,
crossed the Congo – you should have seen
the lightning there! Crossed the Sahara
– quite a big place – went round the
sandstorms. Crossed the Mediterranean sea,
crossed Spain – nice flies in Spain. Crossed
the Pyrenees – pretty windy – crossed
France – nearly got hit by a bus – crossed
the English Channel – another storm, I am
the storm-meister – and all the way here,
through rain, lightning, dark, hail, the *lot* –
zap! POW, BANG AND HE WINS! What's it
like talking to a champ, mate?'

Aubrey got up and stood at the skylight,
looking out. It really was a lovely evening.
He was glad to have someone to talk to
again.

'Do you get a prize for coming first?'

'Do I! You bet! I get to choose the best nest
site, anywhere I like. And when the other

male swallows turn up, the slowcoaches, the flappers, I'll say this is *mine,* you blokes, I got this one, I'm first, and so when the female swallows turn up and come looking for the best nests I'll say – to the most beautiful and fastest bird of all – I'll say hey, this is my site, babe. I was First Back, fancy a look around? And if she likes it, which she will, because it will be the best, we'll get together and have baby swallows.'

'And you'll live together happily ever after?' Aubrey said. 'I wish I was a swallow. I wish my whole family were.'

'*Happily ever after?*' Hirundo whistled. 'Not exactly. No, that's not how it works. In fact, racing six thousand miles twice a year is the easy part, and a lot of us don't make that. Seven out of ten of us are killed on the journey in the first two years.'

'Seven out of ten!' Aubrey exclaimed. 'But that's terrible.'

'Well,' said Hirundo, stretching a wing. 'That's life. You're talking storms,

starvation, pesticides – they kill the insects
we eat – traffic, nets, falcons – there's
a thing in Africa called the Bat Hawk
and it doesn't just eat bats believe me
– peregrines, hobbies, power lines, buses,
weird old men with shotguns! There's a lot
of ways to not get much happy ever after.
There's a lot more "ever after" than "happy",
right? The travelling life is for the brave
and the strong and the no choice mob – and
that's us, that's for sure.'

'Swallows are brave and strong?'

'Well maybe! Some of us. But really we're
the No Choice Mob. I only know one or two
who gave it up. You have to choose: am I
going to try not to die of cold in Yorkshire?
In February? Alone? The only swallow in
the country? Or shall I just get the heck out
of here, chase after that old sun and warm
my feathers in Africa?'

Hirundo stretched out his long curvy blue
wings and flittered them slightly, smiling.
(Swallows are one of the nine species of

birds which smile in the same way humans and dogs do.)

Then he stopped smiling.

'And if you get there and think ah ha! this is better, I'm going to stay here in the hot sun, then when February comes, the South African February, you have to remember well, wow, it's going to get a bit rainy now. I'm talking rain like a wet machine gun, bru! The kind of rain that will batter you into the ground. And you're like – do I feel lucky? Do you? What would you do, mate? The rain they have down in places like Zululand, it's beautiful but it will just *kill you dead!*'

If you'd been watching Hirundo whistling and chittering away you would have seen a talkative swallow doing exactly what they normally do. The boy's head poking out of the attic window would have only surprised you because Hirundo was perched so close to it. The boy heard the whistles and chitters, of course, but in his brain they were clearly English words with this slight sort of accent. When he spoke to Hirundo he did it as you would: he kept his voice down, so that no one like Mr Ferraby would see him talking.

'But that's ... terrible! How do you deal with that – with so many dying?'

'You LIVE, Aubrey boy! You pack in as much life as you can. So when I meet my lady swallow, and we have chicks, and we've got to feed them, we don't just settle down to catching flies all day and getting ready to risk it all on the journey south again in September. No way, matey. We have *fun*. I'll probably make friends with quite a few lady swallows, if you know what I mean.'

'What do you mean?'

'I mean if I'm off over the meadows hunting and I meet a nice lady doing some hunting herself I'll probably give her a kiss, if she wants me to. I might even have baby

swallows with her, too. It happens, believe
me, boy, it happens a lot.'

'But … what about your wife? I mean the
first lady – the beautiful fast one who you've
got babies with? How will she feel about
that?'

'She won't like it! She won't like it one
bit. But when I'm not watching, if I'm not

watching, she might be doing the same thing. Some of those slowcoach boys making their way here now will be pretty handsome swallows. Some of those big older swallows whom I have just beaten can be pretty impressive birds. Strong, charming, seen the world six times, eight times, great stories – And then there's my mate, young and beautiful and fast, flying out there, with me busy feeding the chicks... They might have a kiss or two! And maybe a bit of her thinks I'm an idiot who talks too much – it's true. You bet they will have a kiss if they get the chance. That's the game, mate. That's LIFE, my man!'

Aubrey thought about it. He thought about telling Hirundo about Jim and Suzanne arguing, and how he worried sometimes that they might split up. But it sounded as though Hirundo would think that it would be perfectly fine if they did. He decided not to mention it.

'I don't think I'd like to be a swallow after all,' he said.

'I wouldn't be anything else for anything!' Hirundo cried. 'It's the best. Everyone knows it. You never meet a sad swallow, or a bored swallow, or a depressed swallow. Just does not happen. It's the flying, partly. The way we fly makes most flying look like walking, and flying makes walking look like lying in the mud with no legs. You want to try it?'

'Try flying?' Aubrey laughed bleakly. 'I can imagine it. I can't fly.'

'You could hold on to my back.'

'I'm too big.'

'We could make you small.'

'Yeah, right.'

'Of course we could.' Hirundo sounded surprised. 'Haven't you heard of the Swallow Stone?'

'No.'

'Humans! Do you just forget *everything*? Don't you listen to your parents and your grandparents at all? You guys are so strange.'

'What's the Swallow Stone?'

'Man, the Swallow Stone is a stone you find in swallows' nests. Come on! You're sure you haven't heard of it? It is very small and very white and you have to know which nests to look in. A long time ago humans used to use it for curing blindness. You put it on your tongue and you can see. But then humans found other ways of curing blindness and stopped using the stone. You must have forgotten about it. The thing is, it doesn't just cure blindness. If you hold it under your tongue and make a wish, it can make you very small.'

'I don't believe you.'

'Wow,' said Hirundo. 'You are Aubrey Rambunctious Wolf, right? Not, like, Aubrey Milktoast Whingeypants? I haven't come to the wrong house? Most people wouldn't believe you can talk to animals but that doesn't make it not true, does it, bru?

What's wrong with you? I heard you were up for all kinds of action.'

'I used to be,' Aubrey said. 'My parents aren't getting on. I'm scared they are going to break up or something.'

Aubrey shook his head. He felt miserable again.

'Hey hey,' Hirundo said, gently. 'It's OK, you know? Your parents will work it out, or they will break up and work it out differently. No use worrying. They love you and each other, don't they? So everything will be OK. Things change. You mustn't let *change* make you sad. The best thing to do, when you're worried, is have an adventure. Like – um, going for a walk? Or … flying with a swallow? I know where to get a stone.'

Without waiting for a reply the little bird dived off the window ledge, flicked his wings and was gone. Aubrey stayed where he was, looking out at the woods and the valley. The sun was just going down. High above in the blue were whisks of white cloud. *How can everything be so beautiful and me still so glum?* he thought.

There was a flutter and a light thump and Hirundo was back. He opened his beak and dropped a small white stone onto Aubrey's desk.

'Put that under your tongue, close your eyes and wish yourself small.'

Aubrey did not hesitate. If he had thought about it he might have decided that sucking some sort of magical stone which granted wishes to be small was unwise. He was not in the mood for that sort of thinking. His rambunctious nature and his love of adventure were blazing inside him, and he wished like a great silent shout, *"Make me small!"*

The stone was cold under his tongue. It tasted slightly salty. When he opened his eyes he exclaimed – '*WOAH!*'

The red lamp on his desk had become

gigantic! It loomed over him, the size of a
tree. His *Greek Gods, Myths and Monsters*
book had turned into a cliff of paper.
Hirundo was enormous! Aubrey was about
the size of a large coin.

## CHAPTER 4

# Flight!

'See? Easy. Now climb up and grip on.'
Aubrey climbed on Hirundo's back
and dug his hands into the bird's feathers,
which were strong and soft, overlapping like
shields.

'Get down, really low like a motorbike
rider,' the swallow advised him. 'Dig your
feet in. I only have two gears, bru, fast and
insanely fast. Are you ready?'

'I think so,' Aubrey said.

His heart was hammering and he was
almost panting. He could not remember
being so excited or so scared. 'But don't go
upside down or anything.'

'Launch!' cried the bird. 'Bird's away!'

The next thing Aubrey knew they had
fired out into space. Hirundo's blue wings

were flickering either side of him. The air was blowing over him and the large beech tree in front of the house was rushing up as if it meant to smash them.

'Help!' Aubrey yelled.

Suddenly the world tilted on its side. He clutched on desperately. The world tilted the other way and they were jinking between the tree trunk and the branches that whipped by, and now the valley fields were spread before them and they were diving down, down like a missile, so fast!

'Wheeeeheee!' Aubrey shrieked.

Oh the glee of it, the thrill of it! The feeling of flight was like nothing he had ever known.

They were diving through the sky.

'Woooweeee!' he shouted, and then he started to laugh wildly as the valley tilted sideways, then fell away backwards as Hirundo soared up. There was sky and the tops of the moors, and now they were coming round in a wide, swooping circle and Aubrey could see Woodside Terrace looking small and very stuck to the ground below.

'We're flying!' he gasped, because it seemed unbelievable. 'We're really flying!'

Hirundo turned his head slightly and said, with a smile in his voice, 'Ever done anything better? Absolutely superb, isn't it? Ready for a bit more?'

'Oh – my – GOODNESS!' shouted Aubrey, as Hirundo flicked over onto his side so that the tiny boy was looking down at the ground far below with nothing between him and it, and then they dived.

The field was a great green plate rushing up to kill them until the bird beneath him twisted again and now they were hurtling across the ground a couple of feet up, Hirundo weaving and side-slipping between the larger tufts of grass, which were like lumps of jungle to the boy now, Hirundo's wings flicking occasionally on either side, and now there was a sheep, a huge silly

white sheep right in front of them like a
woolly cliff with Hirundo hurtling towards
it so fast they were obviously going to hit.

'...*SHEEEEP!*' Aubrey screamed.

In the last split of a second they flipped up
and over, crossing so low above the animal's
back that Aubrey glimpsed every strand of
wool. He could smell the sheep – an  odour
that was warm, sour and a bit sweet, like a
scented candle made with wee – and then
they were flashing low over the fields, the
woods zipping by.

They never went straight for more than
a few seconds. Then Hirundo would dive
or climb suddenly, or flick right or left, and
things which were tiny black dots would
become quite large flies, flying so slowly
they seemed to be keeping still. With a snap
of his beak Hirundo ate them.

'Refuelling,' he told Aubrey. 'Want one?'

'I'm fine,' Aubrey said. 'Oh, Hirundo,
it's amazing! It's incredible! It's the most
wonderful thing I've ever done.'

'You get it, boy! So where do you want to go? Up to the reservoir? Down to the river? France?'

'Umm, can we go to town?' Aubrey asked suddenly, 'I'd like to see if Dad is OK.'

'Yessir,' said Hirundo. 'Downhill is *good*. Stand by for Mach Two\*.'

FOOTNOTE: \*Mach is a way of measuring high speeds. Light is the fastest thing we know about: when light pops to the shops or nips to the lavatory it travels at one hundred and eighty-six thousand two hundred and eighty-two miles per second, which is over 670 million miles per hour. Light does the shopping much faster than you can blink, even when the shops are a thousand miles away. Sound is slower than light but sound is no slowcoach: it moves at 760 miles per hour, which is Mach One. A swallow travelling at Mach One will break the Sound Barrier\*\*. A swallow flying at 1,522 miles per hour, twice the speed of sound, is said to be travelling at Mach Two. Swallows often claim to have broken the Sound Barrier. But swallows are not as fast as swifts and swifts say it can't be done. Swifts should know; they spend a lot of time trying. It is a moot point\*\*\*.

\*\* FOOTNOTE TO FOOTNOTE: The Sound Barrier is like one of those red and white poles you see at level crossings and car parks which they sometimes drive through in films. It is an infinite and invisible barrier that breaks with an extremely loud bang, called a Sonic Boom.

\*\*\*We will come back to moot points.

The swallow pulled up steeply, his wings beating hard, banked over onto his right side and dived and dived, as if up to now he had been going slowly. The wind made Aubrey's eyes, nose and mouth all run, and the tears, snot and spit made thin smears on both sides of his face which felt like snails' trails – quite nice, actually – as they hurtled down the valley.

Rooks going home moved above them so slowly. Wood pigeons flew below like lumbering buses as the trees gave way to rooftops and Hirundo brought them down low. They weaved through streets and houses. They shot around a corner, dodged a lorry and zigzagged between two buildings like cliffs.

'Where's Jim?' Hirundo asked.

'He goes to the White Lion. Can we look there?'

Hirundo changed direction in an instant, so quickly Aubrey almost fell off. He clung on to Hirundo and said a word he had never said before: 'Lawks!'

They flew under the bridge, zooming over the backs of ducks, and now they were circling the courtyard of the White Lion.

'There he is!' cried Aubrey. Jim was sitting on the step outside one of the rooms. There was a woman sitting next to him. They both had a drink in their hands and they were laughing. They looked happy. Aubrey recognised the woman: it was Miss Simpson. She taught art at school and everybody liked her. But now Aubrey did not like the way she and Jim looked so happy. He knew Suzanne was at home, not laughing with anyone.

## CHAPTER 5

# Alexander the Great, Yoghurt and Stone

Hirundo flared his wings like two small sails. With a quick flutter he landed on a telephone wire about ten feet above the tops of the heads of Jim and Miss Simpson, which were close together. Hirundo was not even panting. All that wild flying and manoeuvring seemed to have ruffled him not at all.

'Who's that with him?' he asked Aubrey.

'It's Miss Simpson!' Aubrey whispered, 'Shh!'

'Ah, we're eavesdropping!'

At that precise moment Jim stood up, reached out a hand and pulled Miss Simpson to her feet. He said something Aubrey missed but which made Miss

Simpson laugh. Then they hugged, and Jim
kissed her cheek, and Miss Simpson set off,
out of the hotel's yard. Jim ambled into the
White Lion.

Hirundo seemed to be staring into the distance and whistling to himself.

'So that went well anyways, eh?'

'What did?'

'Your dad and that lady. They're good. If they were swallows they could do some flying together!'

'What!'


Aubrey found this exasperating. He was as exasperated as a wasp that has been stung by another wasp. He did not have time to listen to Hirundo's wild theories. They would make him angry, he was sure. He made a decision.

'OK, I am going to get down,' he said. 'I've had enough of all this swallow stuff. Make me big again, please.'

'Big! You sure, man?'

'Definitely.'

'OK! You – want to get down, or are you going to do it here? On this wire?'

'Oh! Sorry. Stupid ... could we fly down to

the ground please, Hirundo?'

'Sure! Hold on! Launch! Bird's away!'


Instantly they dropped, twisted, sort of skidded upwards and stopped on an old wooden table in the White Lion's garden which had an umbrella in the middle of it. Aubrey climbed off Hirundo's back.

'Right,' said Hirundo. 'I've always wanted to see this. Let's see you grow big.'

'OK,' said Aubrey. 'I'm ready.'

'Go!' said Hirundo.

Aubrey shut his eyes.

When he opened them again nothing had happened.

'Why isn't it working?'

'Hmm?'

*'Why isn't it working, Hirundo?'*

'No idea, mate! I don't know anything about it.'

'You do, you gave me the stone. Where's the stone?'

'No idea, mate!'

'It must be in the attic. We need to get it.'

'Sure!'

'And then you will make me big again?'

'Um, not me, bru. I only know how it makes you small. I mean, I'd heard of it. I hadn't seen it before you did it.'

'Wait. How do I get big again?'

Hirundo looked puzzled. The tiny perfect feathers of his red face mask seemed to go a little redder. Then he seemed to think of something and he relaxed and smiled a warm smile. He looked very relieved.

'Bru, I don't know about that. I'm not sure but I think the Swallow Stone does blindness and – smallness. I think that's it. Yep.'

At the end of the Ferrabys' garden there was much activity. Bronko and Pikola had been sent to collect aphids for supper.

'Hey, you guys!' shouted Bronko, 'We've got ten each! This place is amazing. There are so many aphids you can just pick them up anywhere. Where are all the other Ladybirdz? It's like Christmas round here.'

'I got ten! I got ten!' Pikola sang. She had never caught more than one before.

'Well done!' Rodina said. 'Put them over there. We've nearly finished the den.'

Rosso and Zenya were just putting the finishing touches to a snug little shelter under a bush by the small plum tree. It was lined with moss Rodina had collected. Zenya was the most artistic member of the Ladybirdz so it was her job to arrange the moss into cushions for everyone to sleep on. Rosso was the strongest. He had been bending the grass and hauling twigs for the walls and the roof.

'Who are you?'

Rodina looked round.

Gazing down at them from the trunk of the small plum tree was a ladybird. It was a small bright-orange species with two spots on its back.

'We are the Ladybirdz!' Rodina replied. 'How do you do? What a fine place this is! It must be like living in heaven here!'

'I don't know about that,' said the ladybird. His voice was not friendly. 'But this is my patch. You're in my garden. And those are my aphids. It is time you moved on.'

'But – aren't there enough aphids for everyone?' Rodina asked.

'We've just arrived!' cried Zenya, 'and I've just finished the den. We're not moving, Mr Two-Spots!'

'Zenya,' said Rosso, 'be polite. We are new here. We are ambassadors.'

'Am I an ambassador, Mum? What's an ambassador?' Pikola asked.

'Yes you are. An ambassador is someone who represents their country,' Rodina said. 'Ambassadors behave perfectly at all times.'

The ladybird looked very unfriendly now.

'You're not welcome. Get going! Shoo!'

'Tell him, Mum, tell him, Dad!' cried Pikola.

'Let me, Dad,' said Bronko. 'I'll tell him for you!'

Bronko was bigger than Mr Two-Spots. Bronko judged he would be able to loom over the unfriendly ladybird. Mr Two-Spots would fly away then.

'Cool it, kids,' Rosso said. Rosso flew up to the trunk of the plum tree and landed next to the visitor.

'I'm very sorry if we're bothering you,' he said. 'Can't we be friends?'

Rosso was huge compared to the unfriendly ladybird.

'We can be friends if you go away,' said the ladybird.

'Why do you want us to go away?'

'Because you're big, you look strange, you sound strange and you eat a lot of aphids. Go! Or there will be trouble.'

'Well then,' Rosso said, very politely, 'I

must ask you to excuse us and forgive us, but my family have come a long way. The children have flown for hours. We don't mean any harm, and we will leave plenty of aphids, but we will stay here.'

'You can stay tonight,' said the unfriendly ladybird, 'but if you're still here in the morning...'

'If we're still here in the morning?' Rosso asked, looking down at the smaller ladybird with a polite smile.

'There will be Big Trouble,' said the ladybird.

Aubrey held on tight as Hirundo flew him home. Tired, he rested his head against Hirundo's nape and watched the woods slide by. Hirundo snapped up a few flies and tried to make conversation, chatting away about the Bat Hawk, and how he had only escaped it in Namibia by diving into some reeds where he had nearly landed on a baby crocodile, and Aubrey tried not to think about being stuck the size of a ten pence piece.

'We don't have Bat Hawks,' he said.

'You don't,' said Hirundo. 'But you do have the Hobby.'

'Hoppy? The squirrel?'

'Hobby, man, the Hobby. Big black falcon with long wings. Looks like it's wearing scarlet shorts. It can catch anything. It can catch swifts. I saw one this morning near Runcorn. Man, I was scared! Hobbies hunt all day. The good thing about the Bat Hawk is it only hunts in the evening when the bats come out, so if you're in bed early you're safe.'

'Stuff eats stuff,' Aubrey said, remembering something a heron had told him a couple of years ago.

'You got that right,' said Hirundo, and he swerved slightly, missing a wasp. 'Not eating stuff is important too. Don't swallow anything with a sting, as we swallows say.'

'I don't eat things that are alive.'

'Yoghurt? Isn't that alive?*'

'I don't know. Are we there yet?'

'Yup, Woodside Terrace dead ahead. You want to remember though, Aubo, now you're small, stuff might try to eat you. Keep an eye out, mate.'

Hirundo flew straight in through the window and landed on the desk. The very little boy climbed down. There was the Swallow Stone, as big as a white boulder.

FOOTNOTE: *'Is Yoghurt Alive?' is one of the Key Questions of the Universe. Most yoghurt, like all the fruit-flavoured kinds, probably is not alive.

The amazing Greek yoghurt, particularly delicious when eaten with honey, is as alive as you are now, unless you happen to be reading this as a ghost. (Whether or not ghosts are alive is a moot point**. But they definitely read a lot.)

Anyway, Greeks and Macedonians have yoghurt and honey for breakfast. That's how Alexander the Great, who was a Macedonian Greek, conquered pretty well everything he could see on his world map. He then carried on, making a bigger map, and conquered everything on that. To answer the question 'Was Alexander The Great's Breakfast Alive?' would take a whole book, so, for now, is a moot point**.

**We will come back to moot points.

Aubrey tried licking it.

He tried closing his eyes and wishing.

He tried licking it with his eyes closed while hugging it and wishing.

'Not happening is it?' Hirundo said, a couple of minutes later.

Aubrey slumped down with his back against the Swallow Stone. The desk stretched away from his feet. It ended in a drop that looked about fifteen storeys high, all the way down to the carpet.

'Tired, eh? Me too. I'm going to perch up for the night. Reckon I'm going to sleep well! Tuckers you out, adventure travel, doesn't it? So I'll see you tomorrow, Aubo-Wolfo. Don't dream of the Bat Hawk, OK?'

And Hirundo was gone.

Aubrey is now so tired that he cannot bring himself to do anything but stumble over to the loose ball of tissue he used to dry his eyes when Jim and Suzanne were arguing in the garden. He pulls a bit over him like a soft tent. He curls up and falls into a deep and gentle sleep. In this sleep there are no dreams of Bat Hawks or anything else. The moon rises and spreads silver light over the tent of tissue paper, from which tiny snores can be heard.

## CHAPTER 6

# In Which Ariadne Asks Our Friend To Save The World And He Wants To Tell Her To Go Away

The argument in the moonlit attic had been going on for some time. 'We'll be there and back again before they miss you.'

'No! Go away, Ariadne.' His perfect sleep had been interrupted a couple of hours before dawn, and Aubrey was not in a good mood. He had just had the most terrible fright. If you have ever been woken in the small hours of the night by a spider bigger than you are, you will understand exactly how he felt. One minute he had been dreaming about having an adventure with

his friend Jonah – they had been climbing
and sliding in a huge adventure playground
made out of Lego – and the next moment
something was shaking his leg, he had
opened his eyes and there, looming over him
in the moonlit gloom, was a spider the size
of a horse.

Its eight legs were enormous, ghastly spindles arching over him. Its jaws were like a pair of fat hairy hooks, curving upwards. Its eyes were like clumps of dark lamps, all surrounded by more hair and bristles.

Aubrey screamed. He screamed with all his might and kicked and wriggled backwards. Because he was so small his scream was tiny, no more than a mouse squeak.

'Help! Mum! Dad! Help – HELP! Don't kill me!' he shrieked, and felt about for some sort of weapon. The best he could do was a one pence piece, which he held like a shield, ready to throw it at the spider if it charged, as he was sure it would.

'Aubrey, Aubrey! It's me – Ariadne! It's OK, it's all OK!' cried the spider. 'Don't be frightened. I promise I won't hurt you. I think you're wonderful. I'm your friend...'

'I AM frightened!' Aubrey cried. 'Go away – you're scary.'

'I can't help it,' Ariadne said, softly now. 'It's just the way I look. I wish it wasn't. I'm so sorry. Please. Please don't hate me. Things can't help the way they look.'

She sounded so upset that Aubrey paused. He put down the one pence. 'Alright,' he said. 'Sorry. You just – gave me a fright. What do you want?'

And so she told him.

'I want you to come to Europe with me, just a little trip, because there's something I must show you. The insects – the spiders – are in danger. Terrible danger. And because you can talk to us, and because you are so small you can travel with me. You can help. You and no one else.'

'Go to Europe? When – now?'

'Not all of Europe. Just Italy and France.'

'No way! It's impossible. My parents wouldn't let me. If I just go they'll call the police.'

'We'll be there and back before they miss you.'

'No! Go away, Ariadne.'

'Nothing is impossible for a determined spider,' said Ariadne. 'We taught you humans that. If at first you don't succeed...'

'Yes, yes, try, try — but why should I help spiders? I don't even like spiders.'

'It's not just spiders. It's all insects,' Ariadne said, immediately.

'I don't even like insects! They can get stuffed. I just want Mum and Dad to stop arguing...'

'You wanted to know about the Great Hunger,' Ariadne said, as though she had not heard him. 'This is it, Aubrey Rambunctious Wolf. If you don't help us the insects will vanish. The plants won't grow and the animals won't eat. And humans are animals too.'

'You want me to go to Italy and France,' Aubrey said, slowly, 'in the middle of the night, at impossible speed, when I'm barely bigger than an *earwig*, because if I don't life on earth will end.'

'Yes,' said Ariadne. 'Exactly. And you will be the size of an earwig when it happens.'

'This makes no sense at all,' Aubrey cried, exasperated.

'But it's very good practice,' Ariadne said, soothingly. 'You can learn about Brand Management and how to be a Brand Ambassador. It might help you get a job one day.'

'WHAT?'

'Brand Management is about making people like something,' the spider explained. 'Anything can be a brand. Soap. Cheese. Anything. Even spiders can be a brand. But our spider brand has a problem. People are always killing us or screaming at the sight of us and running away and getting other people to kill us. But the great thing – the wonderful thing, Aubrey! – is that now you are small I can show you how we really are, and then you can be a Spider Brand Ambassador!'

'I don't want to be a Spider Brand

Ambassador! I want to be the right size again!'

'You will be. Don't worry. When you have seen what is happening to insects all across the world you will know what to do. And we will find a way to make you big again, I promise.'

'Ach!' Aubrey growled. He felt like he did when his friend Jonah was beating him at Connect Four no matter how hard he tried.

'Where is it you want me to go?'

'It's in the Veneto. It's a beautiful part of northern Italy where people grow all sorts of vegetables and fruits and vines to make wine. And there you will see what is happening to the insects, and then you will understand about the Great Hunger.'

'How far away is the Veneto?'

'About one thousand one hundred miles.'

There is something about feeling exasperated when you are the size of an earwig that is particularly exasperating. Aubrey felt as though he might boil over with exasperation, like a tiny exasperated kettle.

'I'm feeling cross.' he told Ariadne. 'I want answers!' he growled, sounding like someone in a film – or like an earwig in a film anyway.

'Aubrey, I promise you, that's why I am here. I am your guide and guardian. Answers you shall have; many, many answers. We will collect answers on our journey like bees collect pollen. But if we don't go on this journey there won't be answers, there won't be any pollen, there won't be any bees, there won't be any flowers, there won't be any food, and the whole world will look like the moon on Sunday morning.'

'What does the moon look like on Sunday morning?'

'Grey dust. Nothing but grey dust and a few lumps of old space junk,' Ariadne said.

She said it so seriously you would have thought she had been there. 'And you'll still be the size of an earwig when it happens. The moon is a miserable place for an earwig, you know. Craters and dust, and more craters and more...'

'I understand,' said Aubrey. He burst out laughing. 'I've flown on a swallow, and now I'm going to France! It sounds like an adventure to me...'

## CHAPTER 7

# Die Bahn von Zeit und Raum*

'I'll write Mum a note on the computer. We'll have to jump on the keyboard.'

'You really don't have to,' Ariadne told him. 'We'll be back in no time.'

'Don't be silly, Ariadne,' Aubrey said. 'Of course I must leave a note.'

It was hard work running and jumping on the keys, like a kind of nutty hopscotch, but Aubrey got the hang of it. He left out whatever he did not need, to save time and running and jumping.

mum n dad if u back i earwig size ariadne spider say i go see insects italy or world end no worry will b back love u a xxx

FOOTNOTE: *German for 'The Web of Time and Space'.

Persuading someone who finds spiders bristly, scuttly and disgusting to climb on a spider's back when he has been shrunk to the size of an earwig is normally quite tricky. But since Aubrey and Ariadne had no time to waste, all Ariadne had to do was crouch down and say 'Come on!'

The shape of spiders' bodies makes them very convenient for riding. It's much easier to ride spiders than horses or camels. You don't need a saddle – the thorax tapers just behind the spider's head – and your legs hang down easily. A spider's skin is a bit leathery but not uncomfortable, if you ignore the bristles.

Once he was seated, Ariadne produced a loop of spider silk which she wound around her neck and Aubrey's legs.

'We'll be going up steeply and, if I slip down dramatically don't be frightened! Are you ready to fly through time and space?'

Now Ariadne was off. Up the computer screen, across to the bookshelf and along

the top of the books she trundled. It was
an easy jump to the skylight, which was
still open. For the second time in a short
while Aubrey left his house via this window,
which anyone normal-sized would have
found terrifying.

They trotted across the roof tiles. Soon they
stood on top of the chimney pot.

'When you say "fly through time and
space",' Aubrey said, surveying the dark
valley, like a huge chasm below them, and
the moonsheen on the roofs of the houses,
and the sky like a river of silver light, 'do
you mean fly like Hirundo flies?'

'I will let Aloysius explain,' said Ariadne.

'Alo who?'

'A-loy-see-ous!' said a deep voice, and
there, on the top of the highest chimney,
Aubrey spied an extremely large spider
with glowing green eyes who seemed to be
wearing a top hat.

Normally Aubrey would have taken a

sharp step back.

'Guten abend,' said Aloysius. 'Aloysius Wolf Von Wolf at your service. And what a perfect evening for time travel!'

'Time travel?' Aubrey squeaked.

'Ja! I just had dinner in Leipzig in 1742, listening to a man called Johann working on a piece of music. And now I am here and it is not even midnight. How did I do that?'

'Magic?'

'Nein!'

'Aeroplane?'

'Flugzeug? Nein!'

'Rocket?'

'FLUGKORPER? NEIN!' cried the spider, merrily. 'Ariadne has told you nothing?'

'NEIN!' shouted Aubrey. There was something slightly irritating about this spider, as if he would always know more than you, or pretend to know more than you, about anything.

'The web of time and space,' Ariadne said, gently.

'JA!' cried Aloysius. 'Die Bahn von Zeit und Raum!'

'Is it some sort of train?' Aubrey asked.

'Like a train,' said Ariadne, 'only the tracks are invisible. The stations are wherever you want them to be, and whenever you want them to be.'

'Am I going to understand this, Ariadne?'

Ariadne smiled and touched Aubrey's foot shyly with one of her feet, which was furry when you saw it up close, ending with thick hairs and then thinner hairs.

'The best way to understand something like time travel is to do it,' she said.

'Why are you wearing that top hat?' Aubrey asked Aloysius.

He was feeling a bit giggly.

'This top hat,' Aloysius replied, 'is the very first! Made in 1797. I am borrowing it because it is extremely *fine*, is it not?'

'How did you get it?'

'The veb of time und space! So! I explain. Think of a spider veb on a bush on a foggy cold morning. You see all the threads, because the fog covers them with little tiny drops, ja? So. You are standing here now, in a drop of time und space. But the veb that you see on the bush on the foggy cold morning *is not flat*. It is made of a million threads which go from side to side, up und down, forward und back. THAT is the Veb of Time und Space. If we want to go to Italy one morning fifty years ago, we just choose the right thread, slide down it und – POFF! There we are.'

'Can anyone do this?'

'Any spider can,' said Ariadne.

'Spiders travel in time?'

'Yes,' she said, softly. 'And space.'

'So why don't they just travel out of the bath instead of waiting to be squashed?'

Ariadne blinked her eyes and smiled sadly. Perhaps she was thinking of all the spiders that have been squashed in baths.

'You have to be outside and high up,' she said. 'Rooftops are best. From a roof you can go anywhere you like as long it is sideways or backwards.'

'Why not forwards? Let's go to the future!'

'There is no one future,' Ariadne said. 'There are a million possible futures, so unless you want to be divided into a million possible Aubreys it is not a good idea. Angela tried it once. She has never spoken since.'

'Who is Angela?'

'She lives in the window of your front room?'

'I didn't know she was called Angela.'

'Angela doesn't speak and she spends a lot of her time in France in 1890.'

'Why?'

'There are more insects around then,' said Ariadne, 'And I think she likes the architecture.'

There was a pause for thought.

'Do you mean,' Aubrey said, at the end of the pause, 'that if we want to go to Italy and back as quickly as possible – we can just POFF there?'

'JA!' cried Aloysius. 'Ready?'

'But Italy – really? Just like that?'

'Ariadne will explain this and you will see when you arrive, OK? Coolstuff. Ready? Eins, zwei, drei, Vier!'

'But why are you here if you're not going to explain?'

Aloysius seemed to slow himself down. He explained:

'A spider may travel the
Veb alone but if you carry a
passenger you must have a thicker
thread und you need zwei Spinnen – two
spiders – to send you off. It is my honour to
help you with this. Ready? Gut. So now we
sing the Song of Time. Auf Wiedersehen,
mein Freund Aubrey.'

The two spiders put their front feet
together and began to hum. They hummed
a strange high tune, Ariadne's tinkling
voice and the deeper note of Aloysius
combining into notes like a clarinet playing
very quietly.

As the spiders sang the Song of Time the
stars above the valley seemed to brighten
and swell. It was as though they suddenly
came closer, Aubrey thought. The moon
looked closer too, its face expanding until it
filled a giant gulf of sky like a yellow hot air
balloon.

Between the two spiders a glowing silver

thread appeared. It rose above them like
a snake charmer's serpent and reached up
into the sky. In a moment it was a hundred
feet long, then a thousand, curving into
the air and away down the valley over
Rushing Wood. Now Ariadne began to rise
up it. Holding the thread with her front feet
she rose faster and faster until they were
flying along the thread, the lights of
the town flashing below them like a
small, scattered fire. The great city
came and went in a blur of bright
jewels. Motorways glittered and were gone.
Now the sea was below them, no sooner
glimpsed than disappeared behind the line
of the coast, and France was a flickering
of light and darkness. Ahead Aubrey

could see mountains. Behind them he saw
light in the sky, glowing gold and blue.

'Ariadne!' he cried, and he felt he had
barely taken a breath since the Song of
Time began, 'What's that light?'

He felt Ariadne squeeze his legs with two
of her feet.

'It's a Timebreak,' she said. 'A new day in
an older world. Here come the Alps!'

The Alps reared up like frozen dinosaurs,
their spiny backs and rocky teeth sharp
against the dawn. Now they were soaring
down, the mountains shrinking to forests
and foothills. Down they went, the rising
sun warming their faces, and here were
villages and tall cypress trees casting long
shadows. Aubrey heard the sound of church
bells.

## CHAPTER 8

# Killers, Killing, Dying and Death

They landed in a garden beside a large house.

'Wow! That was…'

'Look out!' Ariadne cried. 'A killer!'

Suddenly she was running with all the speed in her eight legs, galloping towards a tall cypress tree. Aubrey turned to look over his shoulder. Behind them, trotting, and now breaking into a run, glowing red, green and fiery bronze, and about thirty feet high, from his perspective, was an enormous cockerel.

Its beak, to a boy the size of an earwig, was a curved and gaping doom. The cockerel was gaining on them.

Aubrey could tell they were not going to

make it. The tree was too far ahead and the cockerel was coming up so fast, its claws thumping and crashing on the pebbly ground.

He made a decision, unhooked his legs from Ariadne's halter and rolled off.

'Run, Ariadne,' he shouted. 'Get to the tree!'

He landed on a gravel path. The cockerel was upon him now. It had never seen a tiny human before, and it hesitated for a second. Then it drew its head back for the strike.

'STOP!' Aubrey shouted, pointing up, aiming his finger between the cockerel's eyes. 'I AM NOT YOUR BREAKFAST!'

The cockerel put its head on one side.

'I say yessa you are,' it said, after a moment.

'I say I am NOT. I am Aubrey Rambunctious Wolf, I am on a mission to save all life on earth, and your job is to help, not eat me.'

The cockerel thought about it.

'Never heard of thees. And don't lika
Breeteesh. Breetessh go home! Viva Italia!
Am gonna eata you up!'

The cockerel made a jabbing peck at him.

Aubrey jumped aside and tripped over

a piece of wood. He recovered his feet in time to dive again as the cockerel's beak stabbed into the ground, just missing him. The boy seized the thin piece of wood. It was not much of a weapon, no bigger than a match, a pale stick with a strange red head. Wait! It was a match! Clutching it, Aubrey charged the cockerel. He ran between its scaly legs, jumped up and grabbed the base of the cockerel's left spur.

If you have ever fought a cockerel you will know the things to watch are the spurs. These are pointed claws that poke out from the back of the bird's legs. Some cockerel keepers trim the spurs. This cockerel's keeper had not.

The spur ended in a shiveringly sharp point like a spear, but the base of the spur, for a tree-climbing boy like Aubrey, was a perfect perch. He wedged himself there as the cockerel ran in a tight circle, trying and failing to peck the back of its own leg.

'Where you gonna? *I keel you!*' shouted the bird.

Aubrey swung the match like a long tennis racquet, striking the red head against a pebble as the cockerel plunged wildly about. The match left a red streak on the pebble, and there was a thin smell of burning, but that was all. The cockerel jumped into the air, beating its wings and kicking its legs. Aubrey felt his grip slipping.

'I hava you now,' crowed the bird, and Aubrey fell.

He landed hard. The monstrous fowl was towering over him, triumph and glee in its yellow eyes as it spread its wings and drew back its head. This was the killing strike and it was coming now.

Aubrey swung the match as hard as he could against the gravel. There was a scratch, a *psssht!* sound, a spurt of smoke and a bright flare of flame.

'MAMA!' the cockerel squawked, skidding

away. Aubrey whacked the blazing match against the cockerel's green tail.

'DIO!' shrieked the cockerel, 'FUOCO!'

The cockerel fled, its longest tail feather singed and smoking, squawking things in Italian that Aubrey was glad he could not understand.

He stumbled through the gravel and collapsed on the grass underneath the cypress tree. Ariadne came down the trunk.

'Brave, brilliant Aubrey,' she said, stroking his forehead lightly with one of her feet. 'I would never have made it if you hadn't done that. Oh, I was sure you were going to be eaten! But you were wonderful. The way you fought that horrid bird...'

'I just want to go home,' Aubrey said. 'Stuff Italy. And stuff chickens.'

But though his eyes were closed he was enjoying the feeling of the warm sun on his face. And Ariadne's stroking foot actually felt good as long as he kept his eyes closed and did not think of it as the end of a spider's hairy leg.

'You were a hero,' said Ariadne. 'You were.'

She said that very quietly, her voice sounding soft and musical. There was a silence. Ariadne slowly withdrew her stroking foot and Aubrey opened his eyes. He and Ariadne looked at each other. In the spider's eight eyes was a look Aubrey had not seen before. They were truly shining.

'Right,' said Aubrey, and 'Well,' said Ariadne, both at the same time.

They laughed.

'You know Mum is probably going into my room right now and finding I'm not there and reading our note and calling the police?'

'No,' said Ariadne. 'We saw that Timebreak, didn't we? We have come back in time by one day. Here it is Friday morning – yesterday. In Britain you are getting out of bed and going downstairs and

making yourself a crumpet before the last
day of school.'

'You mean – Dad hasn't chased around the
garden making Mum angry yet?'

'No, not yet.'

'So we can stop him! Quick, Ariadne, let's
go back and stop him!'

'Ah, no, that's why it's called a Timebreak.
When we go back across it we will be
in Woodside Terrace and it will still be
night-time, or near dawn, depending, and
everything will be how we left it. I'm sorry,
Aubrey.'

Aubrey made a cross sort of noise that was
not a sigh or a snort, more like a bit of both.

'Now, we haven't come to set fire to
cockerels!' Ariadne said, sounding a bit too
jolly. 'We're meeting Signor Bernardo. Come
on – he'll be up on that rose bush.'

Aubrey jumped up on Ariadne. He no
longer worried about riding on the spider.
Her hairs seemed silky rather than spiny
and her skin in the sun was like soft

leather. She picked her way around the curving thorns of the rose and climbed up into the bright pink cup of the flower. Immediately the little boy forgot everything else. A rose is an extraordinary place to be when you are earwig-sized.

'Oh, wow!'

Aubrey sprung down and bounced on the rose as if it were a trampoline. It was cushioned with petals and sweetened with clouds of scent. The petals formed a smooth cup. The light between them glowed and pulsed with amazingly different pinks.

'Look at the colours!' he exclaimed. 'Are there even words for them all?'

'Damask pink, dusk pink, carmine, cherry, musk rose, dog rose,' Ariane said, smiling. 'Rosa, carmine, ciliegia, in Italian,' she added, pronouncing it chilly-edge-a.

'How do you know that?'

'I come here a lot, especially in the spring when it is warm, and in the autumn when there is so much fruit that you hardly need

a web to catch a fly. You can't help picking
up the language, especially if you have
a local to teach you. That's how I know
Bernardo.'

'Who is Bernardo?'

Bernardo, it turned out, was a bee. Aubrey
had never studied a bee up close before,
which is easier when the bee is the same
size as you, and just there. Bernardo was
a bright amber colour, striped with gold
and tan. His legs were as shiny as polished
brown boots and his eyes were like flying
goggles, gleaming black.

'Buongiorno, cara!' he cried, landing next
to Ariadne, buzzing like an old motorbike.
He brushed her on both cheeks with his
antennae.

'You Aubrey hey? Piacere! Means great
to meet you! She tell you how we met? She
catch me! She gonna eat me, but I say no,
no, let's talk! She say OK, you talk. I speak
a little Eenglish, I say to her why eat me? I

am good chap.
You have so
many flies
you not really
hungry. Hey –
you want to learn Italiano?
She say OK maybe. I say maybe? What is
maybe? For sure you learn it, let me go! She
let me go. Now we are great friends.'

'How are you, dear Bernardo?' Ariadne
asked. 'Are you well?'

'I am,' said Bernardo, suddenly serious.
'But oh dear me, oh Mama, we have
troubles. So many is dying. So much
sadness and so much work. So many
funerals, and still we have to get the nectar
in. The harvest is hard. Harder every year.'

'Who is dying?' Aubrey demanded.

Suddenly the day did not seem so bright.
Though the sun was rising gold and the sky
was warm blue he felt a chill, like a cold
draught in his tummy.

'I show you. Look. You see this vigneto?'

'Vineyard,' Ariadne translated.

They stood up on the rose, leaned on
its pink petals and gazed out across the
vineyard. It was planted with a thousand
rows of vines.

'This is Valpolicella. One of the great
grape places of the world,' said Bernardo.
'Makes the most beautiful wine in Italia.
You see the bees working, yes? Working,
working. But not so many, eh? And you
hear? Use your ears. What do you hear?'

'I can hear – some grasshoppers?'

'Cicadas, yes. But not much buzzing and no bird song. Where are the buzzing bees? Where are the birds they gone? Problem is the farmers spray us many times. They spray everything with this *veleno*, this *tossina*. What are the words Ariadne?'

'Poison. Toxin.'

'Poison toxin yes. They want to kill these leafhopper bugs and all these creatures they call pests. But they are spraying everything. They are spraying us.'

'What happens when they spray you?'

'Is terrible. Sometimes a bee gets ill, you know? Can't stand up or fly. These die. Sometimes you lose your memory. You can't remember nothing! So if you can find the vineyard you cannot find your way home. If you find some perfect flowers full of pollen normally you go back to the hive and do the waggle dance...'

'Wiggle dance?'

'Waggle dance. Special dance to remember

all the directions – you fly north hundred metres, you fly east six hundred, you turn south at the old olive tree, flowers is by the rusty car – we make all this a dance. But if you have been sprayed you can't remember, you can't dance. You fall down.'

As they watched, a honey bee left the row of vines and flew towards them. The flight was full of swerves and dips, and the landing on a lower flower of their rose bush was a ragged skid. The bee called out to Bernardo.

'Ah no, Maria, no!' Bernardo cried. He dived down to her.

Maria was in great distress. She was shaking all over.

'What's wrong?' Aubrey whispered to Ariadne.

Maria is dying,' Ariadne said. 'She has been sprayed. She's telling Bernardo how sorry she is to leave them with more work to do.'

Bernardo was beside the stricken bee, comforting her. He said something to Ariadne. Ariadne paused for a moment. Her reply was quiet.

'Wait here, Aubrey,' she said. 'I don't think you should look.'

'Why not? What is it?'

'Maria is asking me to put her to sleep. She is in pain but I can help her. She won't feel anything.'

'Put her to sleep – you mean – kill her?'

'Yes,' said Ariadne. 'I can help her to go peacefully.'

'What about the poison though? Won't it hurt you?'

'I hope not. I will be very quick.'

'But Ariadne! What happens if you get some on you?'

Ariadne did not answer this. Instead she said, 'We can't let her suffer. Wait here.'

'Please be careful!' The thought of anything happening to Ariadne filled the boy with worry.

'I will,' she said. 'Though you weren't very careful fighting that cockerel, were you?'

Aubrey rushed to the edge of the rose petals and watched as Ariadne lowered herself on a thread. Bernardo spoke softly to his friend. Maria was shivering violently.

Ariadne circled round behind her, touched her gently with a foot, and, so quickly and so lightly Aubrey hardly saw it, nipped the back of the bee's neck.

In a trice the shaking stopped. The bee was still.

The spider drew back and closed all her eyes. Neither she nor Bernardo moved. It was as if they were standing guard over the body. Perhaps they were saying a prayer.

Aubrey found himself crying. He wasn't sure if he wept because of the sadness of what he had just seen or because he was worried for Ariadne. He let the tears flow.

When they came back to join him on the highest flower Bernardo and Ariadne were very serious.

'You understand?' Bernardo said.

'Yes,' said Aubrey. Then he said: 'Was Maria your wife?'

'Ah no, Aubrey. Bees do not really have wives. We have a queen, and we all work for her. And we love her! Yes – *amore*. And we love each other, but you could say we all love the queen more than anything. She is the one who is the life of the hive.'

'Does she love you back?' Aubrey asked.

'Well yes, but maybe not the way you think. She cares for the hive. But, oh mama she is very strict! All the young queens, she does not love them. It is hard to talk about with a human boy. Our lives are not the same. We do have all these same big passions but in different ways. Our lives are for the hive, not for one bee, except for the queen. And now I ask you to live for the bees too, for all this world. You have seen

this and I think you know what to do.'

'What should I do?'

'Stop this,' Bernardo said. 'Tell all humans – stop this *now*.'

'But how can I? Who is going to listen to me?'

'You will find way,' Bernardo replied, fiercely. 'You succeed because you cannot fail.'

'But suppose we do fail!'

Bernardo waved his foot at the mountains with their forests, the woods, the flowers and the vineyards.

'You will not fail because all this cannot die. Only some humans are very greedy. Only some humans do not care. But many, many humans are good. They love this world I think. They will not let it die. Talk to the good people Aubrey! Tell them – *they can stop it*. Tell them what you see. They will listen.'

'I am only a child, Bernardo.'

'This is why they will listen. When a child

tells the truth the world listens. Remember that. When a child tells the truth the world changes. Now, I must work. Ariadne – arrivederci! Ciao, cara! Ciao, Aubrey. Good luck! You *fight* and you *fight* and you WIN!'

'Ciao!' Ariadne and Aubrey waved to Bernardo as he flew away.

## CHAPTER 9

# Eric, Un Ver (Eric, A Worm)

Bernardo was barely out of sight when there was a commotion, the rose began to rock and sway, and a spider wearing a top hat hauled himself over the rim of the petals.

'Guten Morgen, meine Freunde!'

'Aloysius!' Aubrey said. 'What are you doing here?'

It was turning into one of those days when the arrival of a spider your own size wearing a top hat and speaking German seems entirely normal.

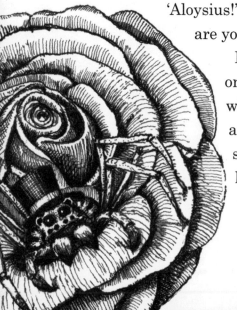

'How are you liking Italia? We German spiders love to come here for holidays. This is a GREAT country! Have you tried Italienisch breakfast? They have pastry full of custard cream and chocolate. A boy like you enjoys this, I think!'

'We haven't had breakfast,' Aubrey said, slightly irritated that Aloysius had not answered his question. 'I had to fight a cockerel and Ariadne helped a poisoned bee to die. Her name was Maria.'

'Ach so? You are emotional I see. When you go on journeys like this you must expect things will not always be easy,' Aloysius said. He put a hairy foot on Ariadne's shoulder, and another on Aubrey's.

'My brave friends! You are ready for the next journey? Perhaps you will find some breakfast when you get to France.'

'France? We're going to France?'

'You have seen what is happening to the insects,' Aloysius said. 'Now, young boy, you must see what is happening to the earth.

Where does food come from?'

'Um – crops? Trees? Plants? Farms?'

'JA! Korrekt! Korrekt! Korrekt, viermal richtig! And crops, trees, plants and farms all come from the earth. Earth, the soil, the ground – this is the source of food. And there is nowhere, nowhere in the world where food is better than in France. Frankreich! Ariadne knows someone there who is a great expert on this. The perfect teacher. So. Now you go.'

The spiders had already put their feet together and begun to sing the Song of Time.

The glowing silver thread of time whisked Ariadne and Aubrey over the Alps as if they were sliding along a zip wire. They came down over hot fields, past farmhouses with flowers on their windowsills and over a canal shaded by tall poplar trees.

'Cicadas!' Aubrey exclaimed, as they landed in a field near the canal. 'Lots of them, and it's hot!'

The field was a thick tangle of tall yellowish grass, a forest to an earwig's eye-view.

'Yes, there are cicadas – but look up,' Ariadne said. 'If you came here ten years ago there would have been bee-eaters flying over and rollers on the wires – big blue and purple birds a bit like hawks. Most of them have gone, so we're safe, but it's a bad sign. No rollers or bee-eaters means no insects.'

'But I can hear lots!'

'Some, yes. Now come and meet a friend of mine.'

Ariadne trotted between grass stems to a patch of soil. The soil was a gold-grey colour like clay. In the middle of the patch was the mouth of a tunnel. Normal-sized Aubrey would barely have noticed it. To Aubrey now it was the entrance of a cave.

'I don't like caves,' he said.

'I don't like the Breetish,' said a heavy voice inside the cave, 'but do I go to their house, stand outside and insult?'

'Eric!' said Ariadne, pronouncing it 'Air-eek!'

There was movement in the gloom. Slowly a pink and hairy worm appeared. Earthworms, Aubrey remembered, looking at this one, have a mouth but no eyes. Movement rippled along Eric's body, his hairs acting like a thousand tiny feet, drawing him forward. As he came he ate, scooping up mouthfuls of dirt. When he

had fully emerged it became clear that he was pooing continuously, pushing out a fine dust-like soil from his rear end. Aubrey was no longer disgusted by Ariadne but he thought Eric was the most revolting thing he had ever seen.

'Bonjour,' said Eric. He spoke slowly. His voice was as deep as his tunnel. 'You must be this O-bray I 'ave 'eard about. No one said you were rude.'

'I...'

'You are 'ungry? Vous voulez le breakfast?'

'Well...'

Aubrey did not feel quite so hungry now but the word 'breakfast' still sounded good.

'We can go to la ferme,' said Eric. 'Oui?'

'The farm? Is it far?'

'Un kilometre,' said Eric, shrugging.

When Eric shrugged a wave of movement rippled the length of his long pink body. 'But we go down ze wormhole and we are there. Come!'

Eric's mouth end looped around and he

began to ooze himself back into his hole, his pooing end following.

'What is he...' Aubrey began.

'Go on, follow him!'

Ariadne gave Aubrey a gentle push. The boy stepped into the dark tunnel, avoiding Eric's earthpoo trail and trying not to say 'Eeuurk!'

Something weird happened then. There was a shimmery sort of flash and Aubrey found himself following Eric out of the tunnel into a vegetable garden. Above, towering into the morning sky, was the stone wall of the farmhouse. Before them were rows of plants. Aubrey was not very good at plants but he thought he could see peas and beans growing up poles, and what could be potatoes and leeks all sprouting from ridges of thick soil. There were butterflies wobbling about in the sunlight and the sound of cicadas was loud.

'This garden is like paradise,' Eric

pronounced. He was lingering on the edge of the hole. 'But in real paradise there are no beurds to eat you up, so we are care-fool because there are many beurds. OK? You are my eyes. You see a beurd, you tell me vite, vite – quick, quick! OK? Oui?'

'Sure, Eric, oui,' Aubrey stuttered. 'But how did we just – how did we get here?'

'Worm'ole,' said Eric. 'Just a leetle one. An 'ole in space-time. You go in somewhere, you go out somewhere else. Best thing about being un ver. The taupes cannot follow. Taupes! Euuurk! *Ah 'ate taupes!*'

Eric actually spat.

'Taupes?'

'Moles,' Ariadne translated. 'Not Eric's favourite subject.'

'I know a mole called Mr Velvet Humps!' Aubrey cried, and the thought of his gentle friend made him miss Woodside Terrace suddenly, and his parents.

'Don't talk to me about your 'orrible leetle friends, ma leetle friend. Just watch up for me. Look for beurds. Euuurk! Beurds! *Ah 'ate beurds..!'*

'Ok – it's all clear, I think.'

Eric shot forward. He shot forward as fast as a worm may shoot. Aubrey scrambled through the short grass, Ariadne scuttled and Eric wormed along, talking.

The boy could not understand some of what he said but the meaning was pretty clear.

'Ah come for breakfast because this is real earth, terre première crue! Not like the rubbish they make of the terre agricole! Les champs are all killed with fertiliseur and pesticeeds! Orrible fertiliseur ... *de-go-las!'*

'That means disgusting,' Ariadne translated, 'And terre is earth, or land. Terre agricoles is farmland.'

'Right,' Aubrey panted. 'Got the de-go-las bit.'

He was struggling through the grass as quickly as he could, scanning the sky for 'beurds'.

'Ah take the selles crottes in the fields and eat it and ah make it good. Does anyone say "Thank you, Eric? Thank you so much!" Do they say "Merci, Eric? Now we will 'elp you look after all le earth?" BOFF! NON ZEY DO NOT!'

'Why not?' Aubrey asked.

Eric ignored him and continued: 'If ah eat 'ere in thees garden for ten minutes ah am fool and ah am 'appy. The farmer looks after *thees* earth, because his famille eats from eet, but 'ee does not look after all les terres everyone else eats from! Ah eat terre agricoles all day, am never fool, am never 'appy, maybe feel seek. Mais oui! Ere we are! Ah can *already taste eet!*'

They reached a long, high ridge of freshly dug soil. Eric snaked into the mulchy mass of the earth. His mouth was curved into a huge grin.

'Alors! Merci, O-bray for watching for beurds. Now ah will eet, and you will go to le kitchen and eet, and you will tell all the 'uman peoples that if zey don't stop killing les insects and poisoning le earth they will all starve to death. OK?'

'Well, I don't think it's going to be as easy as that actually, Eric. I think…'

'EET IS NOT A COMPLICATED MESSAGE IS IT, O-BRAY?' Eric roared. His smile had vanished and his blind head had turned an angry pink.

'EET IS NOT COMPLEX, IS EET?'

'No, but…'

'DON'T GEEV ME "BUTS"! NO BUTS! TELL THEM ALL! OR' (now Eric spoke very loudly and very slowly, leaving big gaps between his words) 'WE – WILL – ALL – BE – 'UNGRY – AND – SOON – WE – WILL – ALL – BE – DEAD! OK? SAY "*OUI, ERIC*"!'

'OK, Oui, Eric.'

'MERCI, M'sieur!' Eric boomed. He was smiling again. 'Très bien. I am sure you will do this very well. Have you any more questions?'

Aubrey hesitated for a moment and then he

said: 'Yes. I am trying to find out about –
something. Do earthworms get married, like
humans?'

Eric laughed, a squishy sound, like
someone squeezing a wet sponge. 'Non, non!
Of course not! We are male and female at
the same time. You understand me? If I was
human I would be man and woman *in the
same body*. So when we meet worms we like
we get together in a beeg ball, and we make
slimes, and soon we are pregnant, and then
we all have many leetle worms! There is no
worrying, no arguing, no crazy relationships
like humans. Just a beeg boll, much slime,
and then the leetle worms. Tu comprends?'

'Yes,' said Aubrey, though he was sure he
did not understand.

'This saves much time, much trouble,
makes many many little worms, and leaves
more room for eating. But the Breetesh, the
rossbeefs, they 'ave never understood love.
If you will excuse me, I must eat! Au revoir,
mes amis.'

Eric turned to the mound of soil and plunged in.

'Aurevoir, mes amis,' he mumbled again, his mouth full of earth and his tail rapidly disappearing. 'Your breakfast is in le kitchen. Watch out for *selles, selles beurds...*'

Now Eric was gone, worming into the earth.

'What does *selles crottes* mean?' Aubrey asked Ariadne.

'Nothing. Now hop on,' Ariadne said, briskly. 'It will be quicker. Time we got into the house. Are you hungry yet?'

'I'm starving.'

And up onto the spider's back the little boy hopped. He was sure he had no chance of saving the world but he was still looking forward to breakfast.

## CHAPTER 10

# An Interrupted Breakfast

The Ladybirdz woke up at the end of the Ferrabys' garden with a lovely feeling of having travelled far the day before, had an adventure and eaten well before going to bed. They had slept beautifully.

Rodina was outside already, sunning herself and watching Pikola, who was always the first to wake up, playing with her shadow in the morning light, making it dance and jump about. There was no sign of Jim or Mr Ferraby, Rodina was pleased to see.

'It's going to be a lovely day!' she said. 'Up, Bronko. Up, Zenya!'

'I'm having a lie-in,' Zenya mumbled, from under a pile of moss. 'Wake me up for lunch.'

'Lazy bug!' said Bronko. 'I'm going to catch twenty aphids, make a pile of them and lie here eating until I am as fat as Dad.'

Rosso was up and stretching. 'Mmm,' he said. 'Hrrrumph!'

'I told you to go away,' said a voice.

The Ladybirdz looked up. On the bank above them was the ladybird with two spots. Next to him was another ladybird, also with two spots, and next to that ladybird there was another, and next to that one another, and another, and another. Rosso counted ten ladybirds. None of them looked friendly.

'Well, good morning!' he said. 'The neighbours have come for breakfast. And how are you all today?'

'Go,' said the unfriendly ladybird. 'All of you. Push off!'

'Never!' shouted Bronko, tumbling out of bed. 'You can't make us.'

'Shush, Bronko,' said Rodina. 'Be polite!'

'I'm bigger than all of them,' Bronko said. 'They can push off, not us.'

'No one is pushing off,' Rosso said, calmly.
'You are all welcome to join us for breakfast.
Let's share some aphids and make friends.'

'We're not friends, you go home!' shouted
the unfriendly ladybird, and he said it
again, like a chant: 'We're not friends – you
go home! We're not friends – you go home!'

All the other two-spotted ladybirds joined
in. 'We're not friends – you go home!' they
chanted.

Ten ladybirds chanting together makes

quite a lot of noise. The blue tits noticed immediately and they spread the news through Rushing Wood: 'The Ladybirds Are Chanting!' they told each other. 'The Ladybirds Are Demonstrating!' they sang, and in moments all the other birds had heard the news: 'The Ladybirds Have Got A Posse Together,' the blackbirds heard, and told the thrushes. 'The Ladybirds Have Raised An Army!' the warblers told the flycatchers. The magpies heard and told the jackdaws, the pheasants told the partridges, the crows told the woodpeckers and the woodpeckers told the owls, who told the woodpeckers to go away, they were sleeping (the owls had only just gone to bed).

Next the hedgehogs heard, and they told the voles and the rabbits. The voles told the badgers, who told the foxes, and one of the foxes said, 'You call that news? We heard that already.'

Foxes always seem to know everything already.

Hoppy the squirrel was on the other side of the

wood when the news reached her. Hoppy
was capering about in a pine tree and
teasing Buteo. Buteo was a buzzard. He
was perched on a branch, rearranging his
feathers, which were a mess.

'You're such a turkey! You couldn't catch a
dead sheep!' shouted Hoppy.

Buteo looked sour. He had just failed to
turn the squirrel into his breakfast. Hoppy
had seen Buteo diving down at her and
pretended she hadn't noticed. Then she had
jumped sideways at the last second. Buteo
had crashed into the branch exactly where
Hoppy had been sitting. Now Hoppy was
having some fun. It was not the first time
Buteo had tried to catch her.

'You want me to shut my eyes and give
you another go? You need practice, buster!
Tell you what, tell you what, try catching a
plane! Try catching that branch again! Hey
– try catching a bus!'

The buzzard narrowed his dark eyes,
thinking thoughts of terrible revenge. He

still said nothing.

'Hoppy, have you heard about the ladybirds?' called a treecreeper. Treecreepers are gorgeous little birds which creep up and down trees.

'What about them?'

'They've raised an army,' said the treecreeper.

'Who says?' Hoppy called back.

'A nuthatch told me – he heard it from a woodpecker. The woodpecker said they're in the Ferrabys' garden, chanting. A thousand of them.'

'A thousand ladybirds!' Hoppy exclaimed. 'What are they chanting?'

'They want the Ferrabys to go home. They say they are not friends anymore and the Ferrabys should leave. The woodpecker says they're going to attack the house.'

'They're in the Ferrabys' garden and they want them to go home? They're crazy!'

'That's what everyone's saying.'

'A thousand crazy ladybirds,' said Hoppy.

'That's got to be more fun than one dumb buzzard. OY! Turkey boy, catch this!'

With a flick Hoppy sent a pine cone whirring through the air. It smacked into Buteo's back with a satisfying 'BAP!' noise.

'Yee-hee-HA!' cheered Hoppy.

Buteo stopped preening and stared far away. His golden feet and their talons flexed, squeezing the branch until bark cracked.

From the depths of the wood came sounds of twigs scratching, leaves bending and bushes bashing. Small bodies were racing through the trees. Hoppy was on her way to see the action, and so were all the other squirrels.

There were about nine hundred and eighty six fewer ladybirds in Mr and Mrs Ferrabys' garden than Hoppy had been expecting, but there was an extraordinary commotion in the trees and bushes all around. The whole of Rushing Wood seemed to be there.

The trees jumped and rustled with birds. In the undergrowth were rabbits, voles, moles, two sleepy badgers, four young foxes and their parents, several grass snakes and eight rats. A small herd of fallow deer had come to the edge of the wood. They were now looking over the fence. A covey of red-legged partridges wriggled through the fence to see what the fuss was about. Even Athene Noctua, the little owl, had left the cover where she normally spent most of the day. She was perching on a post at the end of the garden. Several pheasants were asking each other what was happening. Some of the creatures were shouting at the band of two-spotted ladybirds. The two-spotted ladybirds were shouting back.

Hoppy could not make any sense of the scene. With three skips and four jumps she landed in the small plum tree.

'What's your problem, you crazy insects?' she shouted. 'Why are you attacking the Ferrabys?'

'We're not attacking the Ferrabys!' screamed the leading ladybird. 'We're telling the Ladybirdz to go home!'

'What Ladybirdz?'

'He means us,' said Rosso. He flew to a twig in the plum tree where Hoppy and many of the other creatures could see him.

'Who are you?' Hoppy asked.

The other animals and birds were quiet now, listening – except for the pheasants, who were still asking each other what was happening.

Rosso spoke up. His English was not perfect and his foreign accent was quite strong, but his words were perfectly clear.

'I am Rosso. This is Rodina, and Zenya, and Bronko, and Pikola.'

The family flew up to join Rosso on the twig.

'We came off ship yesterday. We fly and we fly and we find this garden. We make our camp. This is a perfect home for us, safe place for kidz. These ladybirds tell us to Go

Away! But we stay! We do no harm. We not want anyone upset. So – here we are.'

There was an angry mutter from the two-spotted ladybirds.

'Why do you want them to leave?' Hoppy asked the mutterers.

'They aren't from around here,' said their leader. 'They are strangers. They're not like us – they look big and weird. They want to eat all our aphids.'

'Aphids are not yours,' Rosso objected. 'Until you catch them.'

'Well they're not yours!' howled the two-spotted ladybird, 'because you don't belong here. Why don't you go home? Go back to where you came from. Where do you come from?'

'Bohemia,' said Rosso. 'We are Bohemians. But we don't know where we came from before that.'

'Oh, let them stay,' said a big buck rabbit. 'There's plenty of room. There are millions of aphids.'

'Who's asking you?' shouted the two-spotted ladybird. 'Why don't you go home too?'

'This is my home,' retorted the rabbit.

'No it isn't!' shouted the ladybird. 'The Romans brought you here in 43 AD!'

'No they didn't!' the rabbit exclaimed. 'I was born in the warren by the crags.'

'The Romans brought your ancestors

here,' said the ladybird. 'I happen to be
a historian, and you can't argue with
Historical Fact. The Romans also brought
the pheasants.'

'Stuff Historical Fact,' replied the rabbit.

'Stuff the pheasants!' shouted one of the
partridges. 'Pheasants go home!'

(Pheasants and partridges have never
liked each other, because they compete for
the same grubs.)

'Stuff the partridges!' crowed a plump hen
pheasant. 'You lot were brought here from
France. Why don't you run off back there
and eat snails?'

'Stuff you, fatty!' Hoppy yelled at the
pheasant. 'We've all got the right to live,
haven't we? Don't we all get along just fine
in this lovely wood...'

'You would say that,' interrupted the
Historian Ladybird. 'Everyone knows you
came here from America and you drove
out all the red squirrels. You should be
ashamed of yourselves.'

'That's a lie!' cried Hoppy. 'I've never even seen a red squirrel. And we didn't choose to come here, we were brought here, and we like it here, and I was born here, and if you don't like it why don't you come and do something about it, you spotty little twerp?'

'What a disgraceful scene,' remarked one of the deer.

Deer are extremely snobbish about rowdy behaviour. They are aesthetes, which means they value beauty, peace and quiet voices, except in the autumn when they go slightly wild and fight each other. (Deer do this, not aesthetes.)

'Oh, knock it off!' growled a badger. (Badgers find deer snooty.) 'You came here with the Normans and it's a pity they didn't eat you. French snobs!'

'How ignorant,' remarked the deer, 'As a matter of fact it was the Romans who bought deer here first, then the Normans.'

'I don't care if you came from China,' said the badger. 'You're still snobs.'

'We came from China,' remarked a rat, 'and we're the cleverest animals in the country.'

'Rats and deer,' huffed the badger, 'who would miss them?'

'When one is tall, intelligent and very beautiful,' the deer replied, 'it is remarkably difficult not to look down on muddy little fellows who live in holes!'

All the other deer laughed.

Now there was uproar among the rabbits, foxes, rats, badgers, weasels and mice, all of whom lived in holes. All the tension and excitement seemed to erupt at once. Animals and birds yelled and shrieked at each other about where they came from, and who belonged in Rushing Wood and who did not, and who was better for living in a hole, or not in a hole, and who should go home, and where home was.

The squirrels began pelting other animals and some of the birds with pine cones.

The foxes decided they were ready for some breakfast and they darted at the pheasants and nearly caught them. The pheasants exploded up into flight, shouting rude words. In the middle of it all the Ladybirdz quietly slipped next door, into Aubrey's garden, where they began to help themselves to aphids.

Mr Ferraby was staring out of the small window in the bathroom which overlooked the garden.

'Eunice,' he said, 'you may not believe this, but every single animal and bird in Rushing Wood is in the garden. And they seem to have gone bananas. Come and look!'

Mrs Ferraby was at work already, bent over her computer.

'You're the one who has gone bananas, Athelstan,' she said, lovingly. 'I'm busy.'

# CHAPTER 11

# Still No Breakfast

Meanwhile in France Aubrey had to lean right forward, hold on tight and stop himself looking down as Ariadne climbed the rough stone wall towards the kitchen window.

It was open. She tiptoed in.

The spider crept around potted plants. Ahead loomed the metal spouts of huge taps. Beyond the taps, on the other side of the sink, they saw a family having breakfast.

The farmer sat at the head of the table. He was a big man with short hair. He was eating a long stick of French bread, cut down the middle and smeared with butter and strawberry jam.

On the left was a boy of about Aubrey's

age who was dipping bread and butter into a bowl of what looked like chocolate milk. His hair was sticking up all over the place.

Behind the boy stood his mother, tackling his hair with a hairbrush. Apart from pulling faces when the brush caught in a knot of hair the boy took no notice of her. His mother was a strong-looking woman with a jolly expression. She was talking a lot in French. On the other side of the farmer sat a girl.

Aubrey had only ever met one French girl before – Esmeralda, who had unexpectedly come to Woodside Terrace with her parents on Christmas morning. He still talked to Esmeralda on the Internet. They planned to meet again one day. (Esmeralda loved animals as much as Aubrey did, and Aubrey thought she was wonderful.)

The second French girl he had ever seen sat very straight in her chair. She had a book open* on the table next to her breakfast. This girl's breakfast was an apple, two croissants and some jam. Her long hair was perfectly brushed. She had a beautiful nose, curvy like a beak, Aubrey thought, and she obviously loved animals too, because out of the sight of her family she was putting croissant crumbs on the chair next to her, where three silverfish**

FOOTNOTE: *It was one of those books which are mostly words with some amazing pictures, like this one. In fact it was this book. The French girl had only just started it, so she had not reached this bit — the bit that she is in. If she had been reading it for longer and had reached this bit now she would have jumped up in surprise, rushed over to the sink and found a tiny Aubrey perched on the back of a large Ariadne, both staring up at her. Whatever she did then would have changed the whole course of this story, but since she didn't do it … on we go.

** Silverfish are the little silvery beasts with long antennae which you sometimes see running away if you put the light on in the kitchen at night. Silverfish are mostly nocturnal. These three tended to stay up late, after sunrise, because they knew Pascale would give them some of her breakfast. If you ever need a friend, give a silverfish a crumb. It will love you forever. Though it will probably still run away when you switch on the light. Like most living things, silverfish are creatures of habit.

were scoffing them.

On a little table at the side of the kitchen was a television, which was babbling in French. The farmer was watching it as he ate.

'Who is that?' Aubrey whispered, looking at the girl.

'Her name is Pascale,' Ariadne replied. 'Her father's name is Julien, her mother is Marie and her brother is Philippe. Marie will go to feed her chickens soon and Julien will go out to his tractor and the children will go and do whatever they do on Saturdays and then you can eat all the leftover croissant and bread! And the chocolate milk in the bottom of Philippe's bowl – he always leaves a bit.'

The boy was so hungry that he was looking forward to eating scraps, crumbs and leftovers.

'What do you mean Saturday?' he said, suddenly. 'Isn't this still Friday?'

'Ah,' said Ariadne. 'Um, when we went into the wormhole we travelled in time as well as space. So this is actually Saturday.'

'So now Mum is going to my room and finding I'm not there?'

'Maybe, Aubrey, yes.'

'Lucky we left that note,' Aubrey said. He was not really thinking about his mother. He was thinking about Pascale.

Suddenly Pascale pointed at the television.

'Regardez!' she cried. 'Une coccinelle!'

Everyone, Aubrey and Ariadne included, looked at the television. It was showing a picture of a bright red and shiny black ladybird.

Julien the farmer said something. Marie the farmer's wife said something else, and then Pascale, who had been watching the ladybird on the screen intently, said a great many things, speaking fast and passionately. Her brother Philippe joined in. Whatever he said made Pascale cross. Now she was pointing at him and letting fly a storm of French, and pointing at her father and obviously telling him off.

'What is she saying?'

Ariadne replied, 'They are arguing about ladybirds. Pascale says they are beautiful creatures and people should be nice to them, but Julien and Philippe and the television say those ladybirds are pests and they should go away.'

Aubrey was very impressed by the way Pascale was acting now. The girl stood up and spoke slowly and clearly. Her father Julien was smiling slightly but he was definitely listening. Marie had stopped brushing Philippe's hair. Philippe was listening to his sister with his eyes rolled upwards, as if he had heard this before.

'She says that if they do not understand her that is their problem,' Ariadne translated. 'She says all living things are sacred and that it is time people realised that.'

(Now Pascale spoke again, turned, and walked out of the kitchen, shutting the door carefully behind her.)

'She said, "Accept me for what I am, and accept the ladybirds for what they are".'

There was a pause in the kitchen.

'Oui, Mademoiselle Présidente!' said Julien, and then he and Marie laughed and shook their heads.

'He thinks Pascale is going to be President of France one day,' Ariadne said.

'She should be,' said Aubrey.

He thought Pascale was one of the most impressive people he had ever seen. 'Let's talk to Pascale. I want to talk to her about animals! And about Mum and Dad. I think she would understand,' he told Ariadne, excitedly.

'We could...' Ariadne began, but she was interrupted by a loud whisper from behind them which made them both jump.

*'Hallo, meine Freunde!'*

Ariadne scuttled around in an alarmed half circle.

'Aloysius!'

'Aloysius Wolf Von Wolf at your service,'

boomed the spider, with all the boom a spider can boom. 'Quick, out, up, we must make the Bahn von Zeit und Raum! Ask no questions but come, come quick. Ariadne, *Es gibt Chaos, und dieser Junge muss aufhören!*'*

'Hey!' Aubrey protested, as Ariadne galloped out of the window and began climbing up the house. Aloysius was speeding up the wall ahead of them. 'I haven't had breakfast, I haven't talked to Pascale, I liked that family; I want to stay here for a bit.'

Neither spider answered him.

'You speak German, Ariadne?'

'Some.'

'How come?'

'I like to travel. Hang on...'

'What did Aloysius say?'

Ariadne did not answer.

On the ridge of the roof, with tops of apple trees in blossom stirring below him and the

FOOTNOTE: * This means 'There is chaos, and this boy must stop it!' in German.

silver-gold fields of the south spreading out towards the canal, Aubrey knew he never wanted to go anywhere else again.

He would live here, he thought, and make friends with Pascale, and if he had things to learn he would talk to Eric, which would be more interesting than going to school. And when Mum and Dad were friends again they could visit him here and have a holiday, and maybe he would go home with them at the end of it, if they insisted, which they probably would.

'Aloysius, Ariadne,' he said, 'I'm not going. I like being small. Pascale won't mind. She can feed me when she feeds the silverfish. I'm sorry about the Spider Brand Ambassador thing but I'm not the right person to do it. And the Great Hunger, I'm sorry about that too. But I have decided to live here in France.'

'Good thinking, young man!' Aloysius nodded, 'Good deciding! When you have solved the crisis you must do this. Well done. Now, are you ready?'

'No, I am not! I am not solving *anything*.'

'But there is a crisis. You must go home. There is a crisis in Rushing Wood!'

*Just when I have found something I really want to do, Aubrey thought, and a place I want to be, this spider comes along in his silly top hat and tells me to do something else! And why can't Rushing Wood stop having problems – and why should they be MY problems?*

He turned on Aloysius.

'Why are you always telling me what to do?'

'Because, my young friend...'

'Are we friends? All you do is tell me to do things. Is that how you treat your friends?'

'But...'

'And why are you still wearing that hat? Is it even yours or have you stolen it?'

'I have borrowed it, ja, but the hat is not the problem, Aubrey, the problem is Rushing Wood and you must...'

'So you fly around the world in a stolen hat telling people to do things and it's all fun for you but...'

'No, no, I assure you, I am only helping.'

'You're a very irritating spider! You're so bossy, and you think you know everything, and you don't listen to me, and you don't answer my questions, and you never really explain anything. You are a hassle – you are hassle in a hat!'

'Nein, nein,' Aloysius protested, waving some of his legs. 'If I am not explaining it is because I am efficient. There is little time for talking and much to be doing. This is why I am seeming rude to you.'

'What's efficient got to do with it? You could be efficient without being rude and bossy, couldn't you?'

'Ach so!' Aloysius took off his hat and put it down. Now he waved four of his legs as he spoke. 'This is *cultural difference*. Remember *cultural difference*, it is most important! In your culture it is polite to talk about the weather first, and do some gossiping about this and that, and come to the point so slowly, and discuss breakfast, and ask in a strange way, "I say, would you mind awfully helping me out with a spot of bother, but the whole world is going to end unless you could possibly bear to GO TO RUSHING WOOD AND STOP THE CRISIS NOW!" In my culture we are just saying it.'

Aloysius paused and looked at Aubrey beadily with all his bright eyes.

'And so, you see,' he said, 'I am trying only to help you.'

'Well I don't want your help, and I don't want to help you, and I'm OFF!' Aubrey shouted, and with that he took off like a swallow along the roof, sprinting for the point where the top of the apple tree brushed against the house. He could hear a scrabble of feet behind him.

Spiders are quick but Aubrey was a fast runner and he felt all his confusion and frustration turning into raw speed as he hurtled across and down the roof. At the edge he took a flying leap into the apple tree. He grabbed a twig and slid down it. There was a small rumpus as Aloysius landed in the leaves above him.

'Wait, young man!' Aloysius shouted.

'Go away, spider!' Aubrey shouted back.

He skidded down a branch. Below him was an open window. It was a big jump and a bad one if you missed it but Aubrey was not in the mood to hesitate. He hurled himself into space, plummeting down and landing on the windowsill with a thump.

Luckily Aubrey knew all about falling well. He had spent most of his childhood falling over, and he rolled easily, loosely, to a stop.

'Oh!' said a voice.

He stood up.

Towering over him, and bending down, so that her face was close to him, was Pascale.

Aubrey knew that Aloysius would not dare to follow him. Spiders avoid people when they can, and spiders in top hats keep well clear of them.

'Bonjour,' he said to the giant girl. 'I'm Aubrey. Bonjour, Pascale.'

## CHAPTER 12

# Pascale, and the Problem with Parents

The girl was looking at him with amazement.

'You don't speak English?' Aubrey said.

'I do,' said Pascale, 'a bit. Are you a fairy?'

'It's this thing called the Swallow Stone. I sucked a white stone and it made me small. I'm being chased by two spiders. One of them is in the apple tree.'

'OK,' said Pascale. She shut the window. 'No more spiders.'

'Thank you,' Aubrey said.

'No problem,' said Pascale. 'You are not a fairy?'

'No, I'm Aubrey. I live in Woodside Terrace, in Britain...' he stopped. 'I'm sorry,' he said, 'I'm so hungry...'

Aubrey's words trailed off. He felt weak, all of a sudden, which was unusual for him.

Pascale picked him up carefully and put him down on a large chair in the corner of her room.

'You need food,' she said. 'You are safe here. No one will come. Wait.'

Pascale was gone for a very short time during which Aubrey lay back, closed his eyes and thought of nothing at all. He felt free and sleepy. Pascale came back with a small saucer which was still as big as a pond to Aubrey. On it were pinches of fresh bread, some of which had been dipped in chocolate milk, and there were smears of butter and jam and thick wispy pastry plucked from croissants.

Aubrey ate at last. He ate and he ate. It was all delicious. Pascale held a glass of water for him, tilted very carefully, and the boy cupped his hands and drank scoopfuls of it.

When he could not eat any more the boy

slumped back and smiled.

'Thank you,' he said. 'That was the best breakfast ever. Thank you, Pascale.'

'No problème,' Pascale smiled. 'Now we can talk. I don't understand. The spiders — why they are chasing you?'

'Well,' Aubrey said, and then he told her the whole thing.

He started with Ariadne and Hirundo, and he finished with Aloysius and the mysterious crisis on Woodside Terrace.

'I'd had enough,' he said, at the end. 'I dived into the tree and Aloysius came after me and here I am. I can't stop people using pesticide or fertiliser. It's not fair to ask a child to save the world, is it?'

There were no breakfasts being eaten in Rushing Wood that morning. The badgers had become very excited by the idea that they had a right to live in the wood while the rabbits, the squirrels, the deer, the rats and the house mice did not. Now the badgers were stomping around chanting, 'Strangers go home! Foreigners out! Strangers go home! Foreigners out!' while the ladybirds supported them and chanted along too.

'Stuff it,' said a big buck rabbit, 'there are thousands of better woods than this. I'm going somewhere else. Coming, dear?' he asked a doe rabbit.

'Count me in,' she said. 'This has become a very rowdy, rude place. Let's go.'

'Where are you going?' asked a young rabbit.

'Somewhere Else,' said the doe, with dignity.

'I'm going to Somewhere Else too!' the young rabbit cried. Others heard her.

'Me too!'

'And me!'

'I'm coming!'

Various rabbits, mice and deer agreed that Somewhere Else sounded much nicer, without loutish badgers and angry ladybirds, and they all set off. When the blue tits heard the news, they spread it around the whole valley in a flash.

'The rabbits have joined the Great Leaving,' they told anyone who would listen.

'If the rabbits are going, we're going,' said the big vixen, the wisest of all the foxes. 'Without them and the mice, what will we eat?'

'Hurrah!' shouted the young foxes. 'Stuff this boring old wood!'

'Let's get out of here,' said the partridges. 'This is becoming a very unfashionable sort of place.'*

When the pheasants heard that the partridges were leaving they decided to go too, because they could not bear the possibility that the partridges might have had a better idea than they had, and they dreaded being thought unfashionable.**

FOOTNOTE: *Partridges, once known as French Partridges, are very fashion-conscious.
**Most pheasants would rather die than be thought unfashionable. They are not the most intelligent birds in the world***.

'What the hippy heck is going on here, you blokes?' cried Hirundo, landing on top of the fence. 'What's got into everyone?'

'All the foreigners are leaving,' said a rabbit.

'What's a foreigner?' Hirundo demanded.

'Anyone! We are – you are if you don't come from here.'

'I was born here, mate, and I'm from the

FOOTNOTE TO FOOTNOTE: ***The Most Intelligent Bird in the World is the New Caledonian Crow. It does not give a fig about fashion, although it does look quite dashing, being covered in shiny black feathers. New Caledonia is a collection of rainy islands in the Pacific – an intelligent place to live, being beautiful, peaceful, far away from fret and traffic, and notably rich in grubs, which the crows eat.

New Caledonian Crows are so intelligent that solving puzzles is too easy for them. They like to solve puzzles about puzzles about puzzles, and then solve them, too, which they can do standing on their heads. They make and use tools but they are too clever to waste their lives making and watching televisions and computers, which do not make you happy. Instead New Caledonian Crows spend their time talking, thinking, sightseeing, going on little trips and studying other animals and birds, including humans – which, the New Caledonian Crows have concluded, are rather daft.

whole world,' Hirundo laughed. 'Where are you from?'

'The ladybirds say it's not where you were born, it's where you came from originally!'

'Who cares what a bunch of crackpot ladybirds think about anything?' Hirundo

said, cackling, but although many birds and animals felt the same way, and laughed at the badgers and the ladybirds who wanted creatures to leave, it was too late.

The Great Leaving was underway. Unlike humans, animals have no possessions, no belongings and no stuff. They don't need to pack: if they have to move house for any reason they move quickly. If there is a flood, a fire, a shortage of food or if there are hunters around, then animals' lives depend on making a rapid escape.

'Good luck,' Hirundo cried. 'The travelling life is for the brave and the strong. Be lucky! Or be roadkill.'

'Foreigners out!' cried the Historian Ladybird.

'You know what, Spotty,' Hirundo said, looking at the ladybird with narrowed eyes, 'you're a silly little beast who likes the sound of his own voice too much. If I catch you flying I'm having you for lunch.'

Pascale had listened to Aubrey's story with great attention. Now she shook her head slowly. She looked very thoughtful.

'Always they do this,' she said. 'Les adultes. They want a good world for their children, but they make many problems, and they say when children grow up we must make it better. But one child cannot do this alone, even if he can talk to animals, even if he is brave and clever like you. If all the children of Earth tell their parents hey, stop killing insects, stop poisoning the world, maybe they will listen. But I have many arguments with my father about this. He says if we want money to live then he has to make the farm work, and he is the one who makes the farm work.'

Aubrey had never really talked to the older girls in school, but talking to Pascale was easy. She took him seriously although he was only the size of an earwig. Perhaps it was easier to take boys seriously if they were earwig-sized, he thought.

'I don't know what to do,' he said.

'We think, we decide, we act,' she said. 'This is the best way for everything. If the thinking is good the result will be good.'

Aubrey said, 'I don't want to go home. Can I stay with you?'

Pascale shook her head. 'You cannot live here. I don't think they will let a British boy go to school here, even if you are normal size. You do not have your passport. Your parents are not here to give permission. And they would need to get permission first. I think you will have to go home.'

The boy knew Pascale was right but that did not make anything better.

'If only I was a swallow,' he cried. 'They can live anywhere, I wish I was any bird. They don't have to worry about passports and permissions, or school. They live where they like.'

'Yes!' Pascale exclaimed. She was smiling. 'I always wish to be an hirondelle.'

Aubrey threw himself back on the chair.

'Maybe Mum and Dad will be getting on better,' he said. 'Going home like this is not going to be good.'

Pascale had been sitting on her bed with her back against the wall. Now she jumped down and knelt in front of the chair where Aubrey lay. He sat up. She leaned forward and looked into his eyes.

She said, 'They will understand, even if you think they will not, and if they are angry or sad it is not your fault. You are who you are. They love you, so they will accept you.'

He was sitting up now, staring at her. He wanted to hug Pascale but he was much too small. They looked at each other for a silent moment, then another.

'OK!' she said, breaking the silence. 'You must get home! Where are the spiders?'

They both looked towards the window. There, on the sill, on the other side of the glass, were two large spiders. One of them was wearing a top hat. He slowly took it off, and bowed.

# CHAPTER 13

# The Great Leaving

Mr Ferraby was in his attic with his binoculars. He was so excited he was practically jumping around as he called down the stairs to Mrs Ferraby:

'Chiffchaff! Wheatears! Spotted flycatcher! Wagtails! A cuckoo – another cuckoo! I've never seen anything like it, Eunice – there are hundreds of them, thousands! All the birds, all the summer birds, they're all migrating. But now? Why now? Redstarts – and a blackcap! What on earth is going on? Crumbs … there's a hobby!'

Mrs Ferraby was used to her husband's excitements and enthusiasms but she could not remember the last time he had been quite so worked up. She decided to pause in her work and take him a cup of tea. She made the tea just the way he liked it and took the mug up to the attic.

'Here you are, dear,' she said, and then she caught sight of her husband's face. 'What on earth is wrong?' she cried. Mr Ferraby's face was pale and stricken, as though he was suddenly terribly frightened.

'Eunice,' he said, and he looked dizzy, 'something terrible is happening. It's not just the birds, it's the animals too – they are leaving the valley. It's not a migration, the summer visitors have only just got here. And now they're all going. They are all just – *going*. It's...'

'What, Athelstan? What is happening?'

'I don't know,' Mr Ferraby said, 'but I'm scared. They never act like this. It feels like the end of the world.'

The two spiders on Pascale's windowsill were trying to be brave.

'Your friend likes spiders, I think?' Aloysius said, nervously. 'Please make apologies for disturbing her.'

'Have you had something to eat?' Ariadne asked, tenderly.

'Yes,' Aubrey said. He was pleased to see Ariadne again, anyway.

'We are sorry to be interrupting,' said Aloysius, 'but there are great problems in Rushing Wood...'

'It's time to go home,' Ariadne said, reaching out one foot and touching Aubrey lightly on the arm. 'You know France will be here – and Pascale will be here – and you can always come back.'

'They say I have to go, Pascale. I wish I didn't. I – umm...'

The little boy wished to say many things then but they would not turn into words and he felt helpless, and he blushed.

'Go, Aubrey,' Pascale said, touching him on the head as lightly as she could with one finger. 'We have the same spirit. I will think of you. You are not alone. Maybe when we meet next time we will be the same size! Go – your home needs you.'

He squeezed her finger tightly with both of his arms, and then he climbed up on Ariadne's back.

Up to the roof, and along the silver Thread of Time and Space, and over the sea, and over the island of Britain and all the way down to the garden of Number 5 Woodside Terrace.

Even as they came in to land behind the plum tree Aubrey could see that something extraordinary was happening.

The skies were alive with the flights of

birds. Aubrey and Ariadne had never seen so many on the move at once. Swifts sliced through the upper air while swallows and house martins skidded and darted lower down. Ducks – mallard and teal – flew in long streaming squadrons, rowing with steady beats of their wings. A V-shaped formation of bright white egrets with their yellow beaks passed over, following a leading egret who flew hard, as though she was towing the others through the sky. Lower down, tottering along with much effort and flapping, were volleys of pheasants.

Aubrey spotted two Little Owls, Athene's children, with their dipping flight which made them look as though they were skiing up and down humps in the air. Through the trees squirrels were travelling. The undergrowth shifted with the passing of rabbits, mice and deer. The frightening thing, Aubrey realised, was that all the animals and birds were heading in the same direction: south-west, out of the valley.

'Where are you going?' Aubrey asked a rabbit as it hopped along the fence at the top of the garden.

'Somewhere Else,' said the rabbit. 'Everyone's going to Somewhere Else. It's the Great Leaving.'

'Where is Somewhere Else? What's the Great Leaving?'

'No idea,' the rabbit replied, 'but everyone's going so I'm going too. They say we'll be welcome Somewhere Else. I heard it's a happy place, not like Rushing Wood.'

'What do you mean? Who says you aren't happy here?'

The rabbit shrugged. 'The Ladybirds started it and then everyone went nuts. Apparently no one belongs here. So we're off.'

'Have you seen Hoppy?'

But the rabbit was gone.

'Let's go and see your mum and dad,' Ariadne said. 'One thing at a time.'

'The Great Leaving?' Aubrey repeated to himself. 'What's that?'

Suzanne and Jim were in the kitchen. They looked exhausted but they were not arguing: they were in complete agreement.

'It's been too long,' Jim said. 'He does love his adventures and I'm sure he'll explain the note but – it's been too long.'

'We'll have to tell the police he's disappeared,' Suzanne said, taking out her telephone. 'I guess they'll tell all their patrols to look out for him. I can't wait any longer. I'm calling them.'

While they were talking, Ariadne had climbed up the leg of the kitchen table. Aubrey jumped off her back and Ariadne retreated, hiding herself behind the fruit bowl. She knew Suzanne did not like spiders.

'HEY!' Aubrey announced, loudly. 'Hi Mum, hi Dad, I'm back.'

Suzanne stared down at her tiny son and cried out.

Jim looked as though his legs had gone wobbly.

'Aubrey!' they both exclaimed.

'What's happened to you?' Suzanne cried. 'How did you get like that?'

'I sucked the Swallow Stone. It makes you small.'

'You've swallowed a stone?' Suzanne exclaimed.

'How do you – get big again?' Jim demanded.

'I haven't swallowed it, you just hold it in your mouth.'

'Are you OK, sweetheart? Does it hurt?' Suzanne asked, scooping him up and cupping him in the palms of her hands.

'I'm fine, Mum. I'm me, exactly the same. Just – small. Can you put me down?'

'Of course – sorry.'

She put him down and stroked his hair very gently until he ducked away from her finger.

'I've been so worried,' she said.

'This swallow stone,' said Jim, 'where is it? You can't go around looking like that. You'll get eaten by a cat.'

Jim was so amazed that he was almost finding the situation funny. In fact, Aubrey could see his father was grinning and his mother, also with a look of entire amazement on her face, was actually laughing and crying at once.

'Oh, Aubrey!' she said, 'I've imagined so many things that might have happened to you – but not this. How typical of you. But here you are. And look at you now. What on earth have you been doing?'

'I've been helping Ariadne,' Aubrey said. 'This is Ariadne…' He gestured to the spider, encouraging her to come out from behind the fruit bowl.

Ariadne advanced a little and stopped as Suzanne made a sound like a squeak and stepped backwards. She bumped into Jim. Aubrey noticed that Jim put his hand on Suzanne's shoulders and she did not pull away. A rush of hope and happiness went through the tiny boy. He grinned and shrugged. Ariadne made a sort of awkward bob and scuttled back behind the bowl.

'I mean, I tried to help her! But I didn't really. We've been to Italy and France. Do you know pesticides are killing the bees and fertilisers are killing the soil? Ariadne wanted me to try to stop adults poisoning everything but I don't see how I can ... and then there was this crisis here so we had to come back.'

Suzanne and Jim sat down at the table, after Suzanne had insisted on making their son a plate of cheese, apples, bread, butter and ham, all cut into tiny pieces. Aubrey leaned on it and ate, lifting the pieces of food with both hands and holding them up to his mouth.

'Imagine if I had tried to eat like this a couple of days ago,' he remarked.

His parents laughed. They did not know quite what to think about Aubrey's friendship with the large spider but it seemed no less strange than his tiny size.

'Table manners are relative,' Jim said, 'but I wasn't going to tell you that until you were older.'

'You should see Ariadne's,' Aubrey said. 'They are so perfect she never spills a drop.'

'A drop of what?' Suzanne asked.

'The juice inside flies,' said Aubrey, and did not point out that while they were talking Ariadne had nipped over to a web in the top corner of the kitchen by the door – not her web, Aubrey believed – and was helping herself to a bluebottle.

'Anyway, first we have to solve this crisis, and then we have to save the world by saving the insects,' Aubrey said, when he had demolished a lot of cheese, ham and apple. 'Haven't you seen all the animals and birds? They're all moving – the rabbit said they are going Somewhere Else. They call it the Great Leaving.'

'Let's not worry about that yet,' said Jim. 'First of all – you need to grow big again. Can you do that?'

Aubrey looked at his father with annoyance. Why was Jim fussing about size when there was something really worrying happening outside? Aubrey remembered what Pascale had said to him.

'It doesn't matter what I look like,' he

said. 'I didn't mean to get stuck being small but that doesn't matter – the creatures are going to Somewhere Else.'

'Somewhere else, not "to somewhere else",' said Jim, automatically.

'The rabbit said "to Somewhere Else". Like it's a place,' Aubrey returned.

'Anyway, you can't stay small,' Suzanne said, firmly. 'It's not safe. It's not normal. I don't mind the normal so much but there is no arguing with safety. How would you go to school? How would you do anything?'

'I'm not going to school. When I've solved the crisis I am going to live in France. Eric can teach me. He's very clever. And I can learn French.'

'Who is Eric?' Suzanne asked.

'He's an earthworm. He lives in Pascale's father's fields. He eats *selles crottes*.'

Aubrey still did not know exactly what that was, but Suzanne's eyebrows went up as though she did. 'Your French has got better and worse,' she said. 'Interesting.'

'My boy,' said Jim, 'I have news for you. You are *not* going to remain small. You *will* be normal sized again, and soon. You go to school here. And no way are you moving to France to take lessons from some worms called Eric or Pascale!'

'Pascale isn't a worm, she's a human. She's French.'

'Oh is she? I don't care if she's the President of the Republic,' said Jim. 'You live here, you return to normal size, and that's final.'

'You can't make me! I'll run away!' shouted Aubrey. 'I like Pascale and I like Eric, and I like Bernardo, and I like France and that's final. This is who I am. You can just accept it!'

'Aubrey,' said a beautiful, quiet voice, 'do you think you're handling this the right way?'

Above his parents' heads, high on the wall near the clock, Ariadne was digesting her bluebottle. Aubrey took a deep breath. *OK*, he thought, *if everyone had a wise spider who cared for them arguments would be less angry, I can see that...*

'They're just worried,' Ariadne told him. 'Don't make it worse. That was one of the best bluebottles I've had this year! It's good to be home, isn't it?'

'You can move to France when you are eighteen,' said Jim, in a gentle voice. (He could not hear Ariadne, of course.) 'And we can go there in the holidays easily. Let's not fight, old chap. We're just so glad to see you again. Aren't you glad to be home – at all?'

'Yes, I am glad...' said Aubrey.

His parents looked so kind and loving. It felt as though a happy spirit had returned to the house. 'I am,' he said.

'We love you so much, Aubrey,' Suzanne said, and Jim said, 'We do!' and Aubrey was about to say that he loved them, too, but at that precise moment they heard the extraordinary noise.

It sounded like a vast and violent rushing, like a great gust of wind. At the same time there was a grinding and groaning sound from the ground and a shaking and a rattling like a downpour of heavy rain, and with it there was a terrible ripping and drumming and thumping, as if something huge was being pulled out of the ground, as if the earth itself was tearing.

'What's that?' Suzanne cried, and she jumped up.

'Take me, Mum!' Aubrey shouted, because his mother was always so quick to move and he could see she was going to run towards the noise. Suzanne picked him up as carefully and quickly as she could and dashed to the back door.

Jim joined them just in time to see the plum tree lift into the air. All its life the plum tree had grown in the hedge between their garden and the Ferrabys' but, as they watched, it rose up like a slow rocket, up to the height of the roof and now higher,

up into the sky, past the tops of the trees
and on up towards the clouds, dropping
clods of earth and stones from its roots.
Turf and earth thudded down into the
garden. Trailing a lot of ivy and most of
the old hedge wire with it, the plum tree
disappeared into a cloud.

## CHAPTER 14

# The Anger of the Trees

'This is a very strange country, Dad,' said Bronko. The Ladybirdz were sheltering under an old plant pot at the top of the garden. They had just watched the plum tree take off and soar up into the clouds.

'The great thing about travel,' Rosso said, making himself sound more confident than he felt, 'is the way nowhere is quite like anywhere else.'

He was still looking up at the cloud as though he expected the plum tree to drop out of it.

'Flying plum trees I don't need!' Zenya exclaimed. 'I like trees to stay where they are, in the ground. I've heard of them falling over – but they're not supposed to take off, are they?'

'Often in life what is supposed to happen doesn't, and what does happen isn't supposed to,' Rodina said. 'Your father is right, children. The world is stranger than anyone knows. Travel is the best way to find out about it.'

'I'm hungry,' said Pikola. 'Can we find out about some aphids?'

'Good idea,' Rosso agreed. 'Let's go and find some. But let's stick together, right Rodina?'

'Yes,' said Rodina. 'We'll stick together and we'll go carefully.'

The family set out. Rosso and Rodina kept an eye on the trees and steered their children well clear of them.

Jim and Suzanne stared up at the clouds, then at the torn hole the plum tree had left in the hedge, and then at Mr Ferraby, whose face appeared in the hole.

'Did you see that?' Mr Ferraby asked. He looked dazed. 'Some sort of earthquake?'

'I saw it,' said Jim, 'but I don't think I'm awake. I think I must be dreaming. The plum tree just flew away and Aubrey's the size of ... OW!'

Suzanne pinched him hard on the arm. She had turned slightly so that Mr Ferraby could not see her tiny son cupped in her hand.

'I'm awake!' Jim announced.

'Does Aubrey know what's happening?' Mr Ferraby asked.

'Why would he, Mr Ferraby?' Suzanne asked him.

'I think he knows more about birds and animals than most people,' Mr Ferraby said, slowly. 'I couldn't help noticing – you must have noticed – he talks to them and he understands them, doesn't he? Don't worry, I haven't told a soul. I mean I have told Eunice but she doesn't believe me at all. She thinks I'm potty.'

'I think we're all potty,' Jim said.

'Speak for yourself,' said Suzanne. 'The

plum tree has gone and we all saw where it went!'

Aubrey squeezed his mother's finger. She bent her head to listen to him. 'Take me up to the attic, Mum,' he said. 'I know how to find out what's happening.'

'I think we need a moment,' Jim said, and sat down right where he was, on the back step. 'What we just saw cannot possibly have happened. It defies the Laws of Physics. Therefore we could not possibly have seen it. Therefore we did not see it. But – we did see it, didn't we Mr Ferraby? What did you see?'

Suzanne squeezed past him, carrying Aubrey.

'Is this something to do with the spider?' she asked, nervously.

'I need to find Hirundo,' Aubrey urged her. 'Quickly, the attic!'

Suzanne carried him upstairs as fast as she dared. 'Is Hirundo another spider?'

'Put me down on the desk. He might come if you're not here – they are a bit scared of humans.'

'Who is *they*?'

'Swallows,' Aubrey said. 'Hirundo is a swallow.'

'You'll be safe?'

'Always, Mum. Don't worry!'

'There's nothing up here that will try to eat you? You're so small...'

'As long as there aren't any cockerels there's no danger,' Aubrey said. 'I'll be fine.'

Even as he made the promise he realised that he hadn't really thought about things that might eat him and could not be completely sure he would be fine, but he gave his mother his most reassuring smile.

'Shout if you need me,' Suzanne said. 'Don't do anything dangerous. Your father needs a cup of tea, I think he is in some sort of shock. I'll be back in a few minutes...'

As she was speaking the sound came again. It was further away this time, quieter at first, but it grew quickly until it was a bigger, wider sound, the same tearing, rushing and rumble. Suzanne turned to the window and cried out, 'Oh no!'

'Let me see!'

Together they stared through the window at the woods. The two beech trees on the edge of the field below them were rising into the air, tearing their roots out of the ground, rising up with the sun on their beautiful light green leaves, earth and rocks falling below them in a cascade as they rose.

As the two trees climbed higher Aubrey and Suzanne saw other beech trees lifting off too. These were further away, in the woods on the other side of the field, and they climbed into the air in the same slow but certain way, taking off into the sky and floating straight up. Flocks of jackdaws, rooks and pigeons burst out of the foliage around them, calling and circling. Two more trees took off, then there were five, then three more and now it was impossible to keep count. Aubrey and Suzanne stared in wonder at the impossible, terrible sight.

By now the first two beech trees were high above the valley and still climbing. Where the trees had been the earth was torn and raw, showing damp stones shiny in the sun. Showers of leaves and twigs fell from the trees as they climbed.

'Oh my goodness,' Suzanne said, slowly, 'the beech trees! All the beech trees…'

'It's like the end of the world,' Aubrey whispered. He did not feel scared of the trees, but he was scared, scared that things were happening which should not.

There was a twittering outside, a flash of blue movement and a beating of feathers.

'Pretty impressive, isn't it?' said a voice, and there was Hirundo, perching on the windowsill.

'OH!' Suzanne cried. 'Hello, swallow!'

'Hi Suze, call me Hirundo,' said the bird,

with a wink. Suzanne heard only twittering.

'How's that foolish husband of yours?
Want to come for a fly?'

'What did it say?'

'He says Hi,' Aubrey said to her, and to the
bird: 'Don't talk that way about Dad! We are
NOT swallows in this family.'

'Jim!' cried Suzanne. 'Your dear father. I
think he's in a bit of a state. I'll go and get
him. Back in a minute.'

She hurried downstairs.


'What's happening to the trees?' Aubrey
demanded.

'Fine thank you, Aubrey; I've had a good
day, and I slept well, thank you, and yes,
quite a few of the others have turned up, a
whole bunch of swifts and martins, and one
or two swallows who aren't complete losers,
but it looks as though we could have saved
ourselves the bother. Rushing Wood's not
the place it was last year.'

'Sorry, Hirundo – but the plum tree! And

all the beeches!'

'Jump on kid, I'll show you. That's it. Now, hold tight, I only have two speeds – remember?'

'Fast and insanely fast,' Aubrey grinned. 'Can we just stick to fast?'

Aubrey clung tight to the swallow's back as Hirundo cried 'Bird's away!' and launched them into space. He dived a little bit to pick up speed and then shot up and round in a curving, climbing flight which took them high up above the rooftops of Woodside Terrace. His wings flickered as he took them in a wide circle over the valley.

'It's The Anger of the Trees,' Hirundo said. 'I've only seen it once before, in the Congo.'

'But – what does it mean? Where are they going? What about the Laws of Physics?'

'Ha, the Laws of Physics! Don't make me laugh. Humans have only discovered a couple, and only recently. Trees are much older than that. They have been around since before the ice ages. If you make them angry, they go.'

'Where?'

'No one knows. They just go up into the clouds and disappear. When it happened in the Congo it was because too many were being cut down. A whole species of tree just lifted off one day. Irokos. Thousands of them, maybe millions. Just like that – they all went up.'

'What happened?'

'The loggers who were cutting them down were terrified! Drove away as fast as they could. Then the forest people got together and they held a special dance called a Molimo and the trees came back. Look! The Chestnuts are going now! Bye-bye, conkers!'

If the beeches had looked like tall women in fine bright dresses as they rose, some of their roots entangled with other beech trees, as though they held hands, the chestnut trees looked like entire islands with their spreading green, their great boughs and branches, their huge snaking roots and their mighty size.

They could have been bushy sorts of elephants, Aubrey thought. Hirundo tilted and skidded down, taking Aubrey on a wild tour between the rising trees, zipping past them so that the boy could smell them and see every leaf rushing by. Now Hirundo climbed with them. Aubrey watched butterflies flitting away from the branches, and great tits and blue tits jumping off, screeching, and still the trees rose and rose until Hirundo could not keep up with them. They were really high now and Aubrey could see the damage to Rushing Wood. There were scars and patches everywhere. Where the trees had been there was now only torn earth and stones.

And still it did not stop. Sycamores, apples, cherry trees, larch trees, fir trees and oaks

went next. It was as though Hirundo was
skimming through a flying forest, and
ducking and twisting through a rain of
pebbles and loose soil. For much of the time
Aubrey was too amazed and breathless to

speak. He hung on and stared and knew that whatever happened to him he would always remember this extraordinary day, the day he flew through the flying forest and witnessed the Anger of the Trees.

So many went up that the sky was darkened by their great trunks and branches, their billion twigs and leaves all around and above. Aubrey tried calling to them when Hirundo flew close: 'Stop! Don't be angry! Come back – please! Don't go!'

It had no effect. With strange stillness, their leaves hardly waving, the trees rose into the clouds and vanished.

When the last of the trees had gone the air was still a turmoil of birds, many crying in great distress as they flew over Rushing Wood. There were trees left – alders by the stream, and field maple, and some species of oak, and ash trees, and lots of smaller bushes like hawthorn and hazel, but they looked lonely, standing in ragged patches of empty ground. The magnificence of Rushing Wood had gone.

Hirundo turned again and began a dipping glide back towards Woodside Terrace.

'Why are they angry, Hirundo?'

'Beats me, mate! Trees are funny things. They put up with all kinds of trouble for years – people chopping them and pruning them, ignoring them, scratching them, climbing them, cutting them. And then one day they get fed up and they do something. Drop a branch. Wait for a really good wind and knock down a house. But they must be furious about something. All those species! And in normal old Britain where nothing ever happens, too! Phe-ew, Aubo! I reckon you're going to be on the news.'

'What is the Great Leaving? Where are all the creatures going?'

'Oh, mate, now you're asking. I heard a bunch of crazy ladybirds started it and it went bananas. Suddenly no one feels happy here or welcome here or something. Who knows what goes on round here? I only come for the summer really.'

There was a pause as Hirundo tilted over and swooped down, aiming for the attic window. He hit the ledge very neatly. Aubrey climbed down.

'I know,' Aubrey said suddenly, 'Athene Noctua! Up to the top of the wood. I know where she lives.'

## CHAPTER 15

# On the way to the Raven Conference

Athene Noctua the Little Owl, wisest bird in the valley and the owner of the brightest pair of yellow eyes in all the world, was perched on her favourite anthill. Hirundo landed on another anthill, close, but not too close, to the owl. She was very small, Athene, but you kept a respectful distance all the same.

'Hirundo and Aubrey,' she said. 'You wish to speak to me.'

'Sorry to disturb,' Hirundo replied. 'This boy is full of questions.'

'You have been having adventures again, Aubrey. The Swallow Stone? Or just not eating properly?'

'Both!' Aubrey said. He liked Athene very

much, even though she was fierce.

'Ask your questions.'

'What has happened to the trees? Where have they all gone?'

'All gone?' the owl returned. 'They haven't all gone. If you think about which have gone and which remain you will have the answer.'

'The plum, the beeches, the larch trees, the chestnuts, some of the oaks...'

'Which oaks?'

'Um, some?'

'The holm oaks have gone but the sessile oaks and the English oaks are still here. There's your clue.'

'The English oaks are here but the other oaks – aren't English?'

'Indeed they are not. Holm oaks come from the Mediterranean. The larches come from the middle of Europe. Horse chestnuts come from the Balkans.'

'Where are the Balkans?'

'Opposite Italy, to the east, on the way

to Greece and Turkey. The first chestnuts were brought here from Turkey.'

Aubrey saw the answer and he jumped off Hirundo's back in excitement. 'They're all from somewhere else – all the ones that have gone! But how did they get here in the first place?'

'Some were brought by people, some as seeds by the wind, some in other ways. When this country was joined to Europe jays and wild pigs spread the beech trees here by burying beechnuts and forgetting them,' said Athene. 'That is how beech trees travel.'

'All that time ago – but they are still from somewhere else?'

'So some say. A native tree is a tree that was here after the last ice age when Britain was still joined to Europe. A non-native tree arrived after Britain was separated from the continent.'

Aubrey wrinkled up his nose. He did not

really understand why this should make any difference now. 'When was the ice age?'

'The last one was 10,000 years ago,' Athene said, looking him fiercely in the eye.

'So these trees have been here for thousands of years! And now they've gone? And what about the animals and the birds?'

'Many of the animals have come here in the last few hundred years. They are going too.'

'But why? Why? What does it matter who got here when?'

'You would have to ask the ladybirds about that. They seem to have started something they did not predict and cannot control.'

'The LADYBIRDS!' Aubrey shouted, in amazement. 'This is all because of ladybirds? What ladybirds?'

'I know what ladybirds,' Hirundo broke in. 'I met the guy. Small, orange, two black spots, talks a lot.'

'I want to talk to him. Will you take me to him?'

Hirundo was about to agree when Athene

said, quietly, 'Why do you want to do this, Aubrey?'

The little boy was already climbing onto the swallow's back.

'Because of Rushing Wood! Because everything will be ruined without all those trees, without the animals. There will be nothing here, nothing to watch, no birds singing, no creatures to talk to. It will all be empty and lonely and sad. They have to come back. This ladybird has obviously made a mistake.'

'Maybe,' said the owl, 'but mistakes are easier to make than unmake.'

'You can say that again, Athy,' said Hirundo. 'You should have seen this little bloke hugging the Swallow Stone and wishing he was big again! Hilarious!'

Athene looked at Hirundo for a moment, not blinking, as if she were considering squeezing him in her small sharp claw until he decided never to call her Athy again. But then she blinked and said, 'Wrong sort of stone. Find him some green grit. It will be in a wirebird's nest. Small enough to suck on – and wish.'

Hirundo and Aubrey looked at each other. Aubrey grinned. 'I'd completely forgotten,' he said. 'Being small is actually very cool. Thank you, Athene.'

'When you find the ladybirds make sure you are nice to them,' Athene said. 'If you are going to change anything you will need the ladybirds to help you. You will need to persuade them to go to the Raven Conference.'

'Whoa there!' said Hirundo. 'Hold up! Ravens? They're *big* those guys. You never know what they're thinking. And they eat *anything.*'

'The Raven Conference,' Athene said, 'is the ancient way of solving problems. When the gods argued amongst themselves, or humans fell out with gods, or if there was a crisis among the creatures the matter was always solved that way.'

'Where is it?' Aubrey asked.

'In Corwen, on the hill of Caer Drewyn.'

'Where's Corwen? Wales?' Hirundo demanded.

'It is.'

'That's past Runcorn, isn't it?'

'It is.'

'I knew it. And Runcorn is where that hobby hangs out! I knew it. I don't think I really do conferences...'

Muttering, Hirundo sprang into the air. Together the boy and the swallow took off and went in search of the ladybird.


They found the Historian Ladybird near the Ferrabys' garden, where it had all begun. The ladybird was eating an aphid. He was eating it slowly, crouching on the torn root. Until recently the root had been part of a young holm oak tree on the edge of Rushing Wood.

'There's the bloke!' cried Hirundo, and banked hard, dropping down with a lurch that made Aubrey gulp.

'Oy! Mate!' Hirundo chirped, landing on another root. 'Eat up. You're coming with us.'

'Go away,' said the Historian Ladybird. 'I don't know you and I'm not going anywhere.'

'I'm Hirundo – swallow. This is Aubrey – boy. Good to meet you again. Now cheer up, this is the party of a lifetime. You're invited to the Raven Conference, and you've just accepted!'

'I'm not going to any parties.'

'You're not happy, are you?' Aubrey asked the ladybird. 'I never met a creature who seemed so gloomy.'

'They don't study history,' said the ladybird, with gloomy satisfaction. 'If they did they wouldn't be having parties. And when history happens all around them, what do they do? A conference! A conference, don't make me laugh. Why don't you two just...'

'You're the bloke who started the Great Leaving,' Hirundo interrupted, 'and that set off the Anger of the Trees, and you're sitting on a root in a patch of mud with half an aphid to suck, being bitter about creatures who like parties. If I want a laugh, mate, you're the last insect I'm coming to see.'

'I didn't mean the trees to go, or the animals, or all those birds. I was just making the point that those weird foreign ladybirds shouldn't be here and the idiots took it all wrong. They went over the top. They lost their common sense.'

With that the ladybird jumped off the log and took flight.

'Wait!' cried Aubrey. 'Come and talk to the ravens! The trees might come back – the woods can be like they were!'

'History only goes one way, boy!' shouted the ladybird. 'Try studying it sometime!'

'Hang on,' Hirundo said. 'I'm not having this. This insect needs some direct encouragement. Don't worry, I'm not going

to hurt him. I'm going to change his travel
plans.'

Aubrey was hanging on tight but he had
to grip with all his strength as the swallow
shot off like a bolt from a crossbow. In a
split second they had caught up with the
ladybird. 'Hey, spotty! Study this!' Hirundo
sang out, and with a snap he caught the
ladybird in his beak.

'Don't eat him!' Aubrey shouted.

'I haven'eat'n'im,' Hirundo replied, out
of the corner of his beak. 'I've got'im safe,
kicking on my tongue. Corwen via Runcorn
'ere we come!'

The moors unrolled below them like the shoulders of a giant sleeping on a great plain. The plain spread below as they came over the last ridge. They dropped, passing over a city, then fields. Now the coast came up ahead of them, with another city by a wide river, and now they flew under a huge bridge carrying a motorway, and now another, a viaduct carrying a railway line, as ahead of them rose the hills of Wales. Hirundo suddenly gave a squeak of alarm.

'It's 'er! 'Obby!'

And with that he pulled a wild right turn, then an immediate skidding left, a short climb and now a hurtling dive.

Clinging on and twisting around desperately, Aubrey saw the falcon. It was bigger than the cockerel, its long black wings

spread wide, its huge bright eyes on him. The hobby sliced through the air behind them without

 any effort, it seemed, matching each of Hirundo's turns as if it knew what the swallow would do every time. It was coming in fast. Now Aubrey could see the golden claws tucked up into the red feathers around the hobby's middle, and the shine on the bird's beak, which hooked to a point which Aubrey knew was for ripping flesh.

'She's catching us!' Aubrey yelled.

'Diving...' Hirundo squeaked. His wing beats were as fast as ever but Aubrey could feel that the bird's breath came in shallow bursts and his heart was hammering.

Hirundo changed direction twice during the dive but the hobby followed him easily, slicing down the air, its wings folding and flexing slightly, controlling its speed so that it seemed the swallow was towing the falcon, and the falcon was reeling them in.

Aubrey caught its eyes and saw a look like certainty in them, a look of triumph. And then suddenly

the two birds were down almost at the level
of the grass, shooting across a wide meadow
by a river, yellow celandines below them
and the smell of sun on damp grass sweet in
the air.

It was a straight race now, Hirundo's
wings straining for every scrap of speed.
But the falcon's wings were much bigger.
The air rushing through the hobby's
feathers was loud.

*If I don't do something that is the last
thing I will hear*, Aubrey thought. *We will
be caught in this beautiful meadow and that
will be the end!*

'Too much weight!' Aubrey shouted, 'I'm
getting off.'

Aubrey looked up and there ahead of
them was a small flock of sheep. Hirundo
headed straight for the nearest, and this
time he clearly meant to hit the ewe, which
turned and looked at the two birds hurtling
towards her in amazement.

The hobby opened her beak in a silent hiss of triumph. Her golden talons swung forward, clawed for the catch, and then several things happened at once:

Hirundo dipped, the grasses brushing his belly, the falcon's talons snatching at nothing.

Aubrey let go and threw himself sideways, flinging himself off Hirundo's back in a wild rambunctious dive. For seconds, it seemed, he flew through the air. He even had time to think *OH WHOA!* as he came crashing down into the grass.

The swallow spat out the ladybird, which tumbled to the ground, fell deep into the grass and disappeared, and the falcon struck again. So intent was the hobby that she failed to see the trick.

Hirundo, relieved of the weight of Aubrey and the Historian, shot under the belly of the sheep and up into a startling climb.

The hobby had no time in which to change course. At full speed she flew into the woolly side of the sheep with a loud *thump*, bounced off in a straggle of feathers and landed in the field, on her back, knocked silly.

The sheep looked confused. It said: 'Maaa?'

'Ha HA!' cried Hirundo. 'Did you see *that*? Did I happen to mention I'm the fastest, the fleetest, the quickest, the coolest, the Firrrst BACK?!'

Half an hour later, having picked up one grumbling Historian and one delighted miniature boy, Hirundo brought them into a gentle landing on the top of the hill of Caer Drewyn, in Corwen.

# CHAPTER 16

# Surprise On Caer Drewyn

C aer Drewyn is a small round hill above the river. On the other side you can see the town of Corwen, which is really a large village with a road running through it. Behind are the mountains, which climb higher and more rumpled as they pile into the distance. On the top of the little hill is a rough circle of ancient stones. On almost every stone was a raven.

They looked like shaggy old prophets, hunched, their claws gripping the rocks and their beaks like black swords. There must have been twenty of them.

'Arrr!' croaked one, as soon as Hirundo landed on one of the rocks which did not have a raven on it. 'Aubrey Rambunctious Wolf!'

The raven had an accent from near the Tower of London, and a look in his eye of dark amusement. 'And your *swallow* friend, Hirundo, and the Famous *Historian*! Welcome! I'm Corax, friend of this boy. I knew you were a lively one, young Aubrey, but I never thought we would meet at a *Raven Conference*. Hexciting, isn't it? I haven't been so *hexcited* since I was a chick and me old mum brought me a sheep's eye to play with!'

'Hi, Corax,' said Aubrey, nervously.

All the bright black eyes of all the ravens, and their great beaks pointing as they looked at him, would have made anyone nervous.

The Famous Historian was trying to make himself as invisible as a bright orange ladybird with two spots can be, keeping very still.

Hirundo was trembling slightly.

'If it gets too weird you hang on, we'll be out of here in a blue flash, mate,' he whispered.

'What happens at these, um, conferences?'

Aubrey asked Corax. He was very close to telling Hirundo it was too weird. Out of there in a blue flash sounded like a good idea.

'No one knows!' cawed Corax. 'Not until it 'appens. When the time comes we gather 'ere, and we wait, and whatever's going to be forthcoming – forthcomes! And then

we tell all the creatures about it. We're the messengers, see? Hang on a mo! It's starting now though, sure as ducks 'ave heggs – look at that mist! I've seen a few mists in my time, but I ain't never seen one *gather* like that...'

It was true. The weather had been still and clear when they arrived, that lovely time of early evening when the world quietens and birds and animals go about their own business. But now a mist rose from the river and spread across the fields, thickening and broadening like a smoky silver flood.

It covered the town and the feet of the hills. The ravens began to caw and croak to each other as the mist still thickened and swelled up towards them.

The ravens all had the same accent as Corax: it was like listening to a large family, very throaty and very rough-voiced, with their own peculiar language.

'Would you Adam and Eve it!'

'I've 'eard of this but I ain't 'eard of no one who seen it!'

'You know what this could mean, doncha? Well, doncha?'

'*SHE'S never* going to turn up?'

'Nah! It's only 'appened, what – as it ever 'appened?'

'She is, you know – this is how it goes – Great grandad told me when I was a squabbling – the mist – and then she comes!'

'You're 'avin a laugh, sister! You're pulling my beak. She's not going to show – she never shows. It's a story.'

'Oh yeah? Well I've got a whole dead cow, fresh as a daisy, which says she's coming and she's coming now! Fancy the wager do ya, bruv?'

'An 'ole cow? I'm not sure now, that's a lot of loot that is, an 'ole cow... You reckon? You really, really reckon?'

'I know it, bruv, I know it, I won't even take yer mangy ol' cow, I'd be robbin' yer.'

'OI! Everybody stow yer rattlin'!' Corax rasped. 'It's the time. Can't you tell? It's the silence. It's the stillness. Any second now...'

There was a silence such as Aubrey had never known. The mist has ceased to rise. It lay, thick and white and over everything except the top of the hill, as if a tide of cloud had covered the world up to the edge of the stones.

Only the mountains rode above the mist, like an island on a silent sea. Below, in the mist, no car drove, no dog barked, no bird sang. The skies above were empty and still, a strange and faded silver blue.

And then, to the north, where Aubrey knew the coast must be, a smooth round shape broke through the mist like a sea creature surfacing. It was huge, Aubrey saw, almost unimaginably huge. At first it looked like an upside-down boat, like the upturned hull of a vast and mighty ship, and then it was a dome – the most enormous dome, a dome that could cover a city easily – and still it came up out of the cloud, bigger and bigger and Aubrey saw it had a swirl in it, a whorl, a spiral shape, like a...

*No*! he thought. *It can't be.*

The ravens' beaks hung open in amazement. In front of the great spiral dome, which was still growing, still swelling, still lifting out of the mist and towering massively above them now, in front of it and much nearer to them – right next to the hill in fact – was something that looked at first like the glistening silver neck of a sea monster. Like a serpent it rose above them, and now it was pronged. Two thinner necks sprouted from the first, and on the end of each was...

*It just can't be*! Aubrey marvelled. *No way! It isn't...!*

But it was.

It was not a dome. It was
a gigantic, colossal shell.
And it was not a sea
monster's neck. On the
end of the two stalks at
the top of the neck were two
mighty grey-green orbs, each
the size of a stadium. They blinked. Out of
the mist had risen a snail as big as the sky.

The neck flexed and now the two vast gentle
eyes were hanging over them all.

'Hello, ravens,' said the snail, in an
amazingly quiet voice.

'Your Slowness!' croaked Corax, 'Your
Great Grey Slowness!'

'Corax, hello. Coraxes, hello. Aubrey,
hello. Hirundo, hello. And Herodotus, hello
to you.'

The ladybird squeaked, 'You know my
name!'

'Of course she knows your name, you dipper, it's the Great Grey Slowness Herself!' Corax squawked. 'The Universal Snail! The Height of Height, the Depth of Depth, the All-Time Time! She knows all there is to be known, you ignorant bug, bow down!'

'Let's not get overexcited,' said the snail. 'No formalities, no name-calling. Rather disapprove of all that.'

'No! Yes! Of course. Sorry!'

'So-oh,' said the Great Grey Slowness, 'would you like to tell me *all* about it?'

No bird or ladybird spoke.

The snail turned its eyeballs on Aubrey. Strangely, he did not feel nervous. He felt light and calm and happy, as if he had never had a trouble in the world, as if all was well everywhere, with everyone, for all time. It was a peculiar sensation and it made him smile.

'Are you – like – *God*?' Aubrey heard himself ask the creature.

'A bit like,' said the snail, slowly. 'A version, you could say. Immortal and all-knowing, sort of thing. Didn't make the world or anything. Nothing to do with religion. No worshippers or followers, just a few responsibilities. Lots of planets in all the universes. Not bad if you take it slow.'

'If you're all-knowing,' Aubrey grinned, 'shouldn't you be telling us *all* about it?'

'Like to hear it from the parties involved,' said the snail.

'This ladybird is interested in history,' Hirundo piped up. 'He told a bunch of other ladybirds to go home, then told a lot of other woodfolk they didn't come from Rushing Wood either. They all packed up, and half the trees went up into the clouds. Not much left of the wood, and everything in a tizz.'

'Well put,' said the snail. 'True, isn't it,

Herodotus?'

'Yes,' said the ladybird. 'But isn't it true that everything comes from somewhere? And if things just go wherever they want, it's chaos. Everything should stay where it's from, shouldn't it?'

'That's not all!' Aubrey exclaimed. 'I travelled the web of time and space, and I saw how humans are poisoning the earth and the insects, and Ariadne says if we don't stop it, the Great Hunger will come. Can you, erm, troubleshoot ... everything?'

'I can, as it happens,' said the snail, thoughtfully. 'What you see is me at about one hundred billionth magnification. When planets get out of balance I Grub Up. Always a pity. But better than great imbalance.'

'What does that mean?' Aubrey said, still feeling absolutely relaxed, although he had a funny feeling he knew what was coming, and that it was not good news. 'How do you Grub Up imbalance?'

'Great Imbalance is when there are more ill and unhappy living things on a planet then there are healthy and happy ones. That's Grub Up.'

'What happens?'

'I grow to a hundred billion times this size and eat,' said the snail, gently. 'Down in one. No one feels a thing. The end. Save you all the Great Hunger, and the toxins, and the poison, and the disease. I jump to the main course and that's that.'

'You mean – you swallow us? Everything?'

'Yup. The planet, or the solar system, however far you guys have spread – OWP!'

Aubrey stared at the snail in amazement. The snail stared back.

'But ... but how do you decide about Grubbing Up?'

'I don't. It's all maths,' the snail confided. 'I just keep an eye on the numbers.'

'How does it look at the moment?'

'Getting pretty close,' the snail admitted. 'I rather dread checking. But if the trees are going, if the animals can't live together, if the insects are being poisoned, then – well, *ULP!*'

The ravens looked at one another. Aubrey could not think of any more questions. Hirundo ruffled his feathers uneasily. Then the ladybird spoke.

'What I want to know is, am I right or wrong? Wouldn't everyone be happier if everything just lived in the place that it came from?'

The snail seemed to think about this.

'Easier to understand if I show you,' she said. 'Ever heard of the Universal Map?'

Aubrey shook his head. Hirundo, Herodotus and all the ravens shook their heads.

'Right, this is Earth, where you live,' said the snail, and a glowing green-blue dot the size of a marble appeared just above them. 'And here are the other planets in your solar system.'

Red, gold, blue and white, other dots appeared, Saturn with its rings and Jupiter larger and red: a big marble.

'Easier to see when it's dark,' said the snail, and Aubrey felt a feeling like a squeeze all through him, and the sky darkened as if the sun had suddenly gone down. Now all the coloured dots glowed and flashed with the brilliance of stars. Above them the sky was clear, and the real stars glittered in a clear, still night.

'Here's the sun.'

A glowing golden orb the size of an orange now hung in the air, and the planets began to revolve around it.

'Now supposing you could stand back a bit. This is your galaxy,' said the snail. The air above the hilltop was filled with a spray of dots and lights and tiny shining sparks and little winking fires, and there were flashes of light and sparkles of colour dancing between them, and they formed a glittering spiral filling the air, a spiral made of a hundred billion shimmering specks.

'That's where you live. Place called the Milky Way. Can anyone see Earth? Or the sun? They're in there – somewhere. No? OK, we'll go back a bit more. Here's some more galaxies.'

'It's so beautiful,' Aubrey whispered. 'It's unbelievably beautiful!'

All the ravens, the swallow and the ladybird were gaping at the sight, as though the miraculous colours and sparks, the million tiny planets had bewitched them.

'Yes, Infernal Beauty,' said the snail, gently.

'Infernal,' Aubrey repeated, dreamily. 'Hey,' he said, 'wait, doesn't that mean like hell?'

'Yes. Infernal, underground. But in your Old French, infini, the shades. Look *up*.'

Aubrey tilted his head back and looked up. Above the shimmering of the tiny dot galaxies that the snail had conjured the stars were shining in the sudden night, a night which Aubrey was sure had fallen on Corwen, or been drawn down somehow by the snail, in the middle of the late afternoon.

'You see the Seven Sisters, the Pleiades?'

The snail nodded one giant eye on its towering tentacle of a neck towards a shape of bright stars.

'Look at them hard. Now look at the darkness, the shades in between them. Do you see how bright they flash, their colours, when you are looking at the shades? That is Infernal Beauty. Infini and Lumine, the Eternal Twins.'

Now the huge, hilltop-sized spiral of lights just above them shrank to a small white spot, and at the same time the air filled with hundreds, thousands, then millions, then billions of bright spots. Like a spray of fairy lights the tiny galaxies twinkled, all shrinking to points of light. They winked like fractions of stars. Now they spread out across the sky as far as you could see.

The birds, the boy and the ladybird gazed.

'Two thousand billion galaxies,' said the snail, in a calm voice. 'And in just one of them, a hundred billion planets. And on just one of *them*, you lot. Now, I am going to ask you all a question. Does it *matter* which bit of that tiny, tiny *speck* you tiny, tiny little specks *come from?*'

The snail's two colossal eyes lowered down out of the sky towards them. They had a milky, silvery look, Aubrey thought, the eyeballs.

Aubrey drew breath. Hirundo cocked his head. Herodotus the Historian Ladybird started to raise one of his feet.

'To Love And To Help is the Universal Law. And I'm not really interested in your words. I am very interested in your deeds. From now on, imagine the universe is watching you.'

225

The snail barely paused. 'I think you've all got the answer, so here's the next question. What can you do to make sure I don't have to *chomp* you all up?'

There was a pause for thought.

'It's mostly the humans' fault,' Herodotus said, after the pause. 'They do the most damage.'

The snail's great eyes turned on Aubrey.

'True, Aubrey?'

'Yes... But... We also do the most good!'

'Oh, nonsense!' cried the ladybird. 'Like what?'

'We have hospitals, and vets, and animal rescue centres, and um, universities, and libraries, and schools, and we make music, we make great cheese...'

'Everyone makes music,' said the ladybird.

'And we make beautiful things like, um, cathedrals, cars, no! Um, and poems and plays and books and paintings and...'

'You could do a lot better, mate,' said Hirundo. 'The way you guys treat the world and each other – it's not great, is it?'

'Well,' said Aubrey, looking at his friend. 'No?'

'If you would only tell the humans you'll *chomp* them, I am sure they would try much harder,' Hirundo said to the snail. 'Can you just chomp the humans and leave the rest of us, bru?'

The snail looked at him for a long moment.

Aubrey felt less happy and relaxed now, he realised.

'That would solve the problem,' said Herodotus the Historian Ladybird. 'The Earth without humans would be paradise! Grub them up, Oh Mighty Slowness!'

'Maybe I should,' said the snail. 'Will anyone speak in their defence?'

The ravens looked at each other. Corax said, 'Apart from Aubrey I don't really know any. Can't say they've been much help to ravens, over the years. Some of them shoot

at us.'

'Historically speaking,' said the Historian, 'Humans are dreadful! They destroy everything. There are too many of them. You should grub up half of them at least – the big half. They chop down forests, they poison the air, they poison the soil, they are very bad for insects, animals, birds and fish. And plants.'

'You make a good prosecutor,' said the snail. 'Will any speak in their defence? Well, *Hirundo Rustica*, barn swallow,' the snail continued, 'You nest on human houses and you live near humans, and you see a lot of them on your travels. Do you think they can do better?'

Hirundo shuffled from foot to foot and ruffled his feathers.

In all their travels Aubrey had never seen Hirundo lost for words. And Hirundo, he saw, was not lost for them now.

'The thing I like about humans?' Hirundo

said. 'When they get together to watch
something they like they are so full of love.
They have huge concerts. Hundreds of
thousands of humans singing and dancing.
I met a theatre mouse once, said they have
the most amazing plays and concerts! They
sing and pray to their gods. They read to
children and play with them, they cheer
at games – they love making a noise! And
they hug each other and balls get kicked
into nets or hit with bats. They do a lot of
damage – you know they do,' he said to
Aubrey. 'But I think you mean well. Don't
you? You are very loving. I would be quite
sorry to see you go.'

'Thanks,' said Aubrey, after a moment,
feeling oddly embarrassed.

'Do you have anything to add, Aubrey
Rambunctious Wolf? What will you say in
defence of humankind?'

'Um,' said Aubrey. With the eyes of all the
ravens, the ladybird, the swallow and the

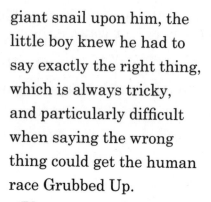

giant snail upon him, the little boy knew he had to say exactly the right thing, which is always tricky, and particularly difficult when saying the wrong thing could get the human race Grubbed Up.

'Um, we – we do love animals. And we love the earth, we do. It's just that we get greedy, and' – he thought of his father and Mr Ferraby charging around in the garden hunting ladybirds – 'we can be dangerous. But we can be better! We will be better, I'm sure. Especially if people knew they could be grubbed up, I'm sure they would try much harder to be good.'

'It is a fair point,' said the snail, 'humans are very loving. All creatures are. So I will pass judgment: the humans may have One Last Chance. But, Aubrey Rambunctious

Wolf, if they hear the message and don't change their ways, either they have not understood it or they do not care. You will make sure they understand?'

Aubrey slightly quailed inside. (This means, inside he felt like a quail looks when it is frightened: they shrink down and slightly shiver.)

'As much as you can,' the snail added. 'I don't expect you to change them all at once: just speak to any who will listen.'

'OK,' said Aubrey.

'Does this mean...?' the ladybird began, timidly.

'You've seen the Universal Map. You are all living on a speck of dust and light. You know nothing about anything but you can see the universe whenever you look up. All you know is, you are all here. So go back to Rushing Wood, and start loving each other and helping each other. Ravens, you have the message?'

Corax cried: 'We have it, Your Slowness!

We will pass on the message.'

'Good. Thank you.'

'You're good, Slowcoach old mate,' said Hirundo. 'That was a great speech, made perfect sense. I'm going to tell every bird I meet I saw you! I'll say what you said, and I'll love everyone who lets me, and I'll help wherever I can.'

'I'm sure you will,' said the snail. 'Good luck. Now, anyone who hears the message has a great responsibility to spread it, and to set an example. I will be watching. My hopes are with you. Until the end of time – goodbye.'

'Just before you go!' shouted Aubrey, 'One thing! Actually – a couple of things!'

The snail had started to draw back its neck, its eyes lifting away on the end of their stalks as the mighty shell began to sink into the mist.

'Yes, Aubrey?' it said.

'Um, do you know where I can find a

wirebird?'

'I do,' said the snail. 'The wirebird is a species of plover which lives only in one place on earth.'

'Where's that?'

'It's a small island over a thousand miles off the coast of Angola in the middle of the South Atlantic Ocean,' said the snail. 'It's called Saint Helena.'

'Saint Helena!' Aubrey yelled, and he burst out laughing. 'How am I going to get there without driving my parents crazy and missing school and everything? Even if Ariadne will come!'

'It's a moot point,' said the snail, and winked.* 'But maybe if you go home now and get a good night's sleep things will look different in the morning. You might find you look quite different yourself.'

'And!' shouted Aubrey, bubbling with the big questions he should have asked the snail, 'Can you tell us – what is the meaning

---

FOOTNOTE: *I told you we would come back to moot points.

of life? Are you God? What happens after death? What happens if you go to the edge of the universe? Is there life on other planets?'

But the snail had already drawn back. As Aubrey watched, the huge creature disappeared into the mist.

'Unbelievable,' said the little boy. 'Why didn't I ask that first?'

## CHAPTER 17

# A Wonderful End to the Holidays

'Well, seeing as you're not from round here, you probably need a bit of help moving in,' Herodotus said to Rosso. 'You've got that shelter in the wrong place. When it rains the water comes right down there, see? It will wash you away. Follow me. And bring Bronko. He looks like he could do with some exercise. I'll show you some better places.'

'You – are – very – kind!' exclaimed Rosso, with something like complete disbelief.

'Thank you!' called his wife. 'I'm Rodina, by the way, and these are...'

'Your daughters, Zenya and Pikola, I know. I'm Herodotus. Pleased to um, anyway, best get on...'

Aubrey lay in the garden, lazing in the first really warm sun of the year, and watched as Bronko followed Rosso who followed Herodotus as he took off and flew up past the plum tree.

In the night all the trees had returned. No one heard them come back. No one saw them. People like Jim and Suzanne and Mr Ferraby who had watched them take off now doubted that they had really seen what they thought, yesterday, that they did see. It was like a dream, or a nightmare, or a strange vision, not reality.

Reality was waking up in the morning on the last day of the Easter holidays and looking out of the window and seeing all the beautiful sunlit greens of the young beech leaves just where they should be, and all the chestnuts, sycamores, larches, cherries and oaks exactly where they had always been, too.

Mr Ferraby looked keenly out of his attic window, observing everything, and he saw that the birds were flitting between the trees, and that the animals were out and about too: he spotted two rabbits lolloping along the edge of the wood, and as he watched a grey squirrel appeared on one of the posts at the top of Aubrey's garden and chittered.

In the kitchen Jim was spreading butter on toast for a late breakfast and Suzanne was standing behind him with her arms around his waist. They were both giggling at something Suzanne had said. His parents were very loving this morning, Aubrey thought. Whatever had made them annoyed with each other seemed to have passed and gone.

Aubrey went up to the top of his garden. Mr Ferraby turned away and went downstairs, because he did not like to spy on Aubrey when the boy talked to animals.

'What you got in your hand, Bree?' asked
Hoppy.

'This is Ariadne,' Aubrey said. 'She lives
with us.'

'Nice legs,' Hoppy said, 'and nice eyes. And
what a lot of them! So you guys been up to
anything interesting?'

'Nothing special,' said Aubrey. 'We
travelled a bit. I went to Wales yesterday,
got back last night. I was feeling a bit small
and strange when I went to bed, and I had
a dream about a snail, but when I woke up
this morning and I was – I was me again!'

'I was hoping we might go on a little trip,'
Ariadne said. 'We were thinking of going
to the seaside near Jamestown, but then
Aubrey woke up this morning in his own
bed, quite a different person! Very stay-at-
home.'

She winked at Aubrey with several of her
eyes.

Hoppy wrinkled up her nose. 'Doesn't

sound like him. How come everybody's a bit strange this morning? They're all being nice to each other! You know I told a crow he was a bag of bad bones and all he did was say "Har"? Normally those guys go wild. Jamestown? Where is that?' Hoppy asked, gnawing on a green hazelnut.

'Euch, it's nowhere near ripe,' she said to herself. 'Where's that whacky ladybird? I'll bung it at him.'

'You know, Hoppy, Herodotus is actually not a bad bug at all,' Aubrey said. 'He's helping the ladybirdz settle in.'

'All ladybirds are whackos,' Hoppy said, 'All the insects are – bonkers! Not spiders, obviously, Ariadne. No offence.'

'Coming from a squirrel it's a compliment,' Ariadne said, sweetly. 'Jamestown is on St Helena,' she added.

'Nice place?' Hoppy asked.

'I don't know,' Ariadne said, 'I've never been.'

'Well give me a shout if you decide to go,'

Hoppy said. 'Might come with you. Right, I'm going to go wind up that buzzard. Surely someone's going to be up for a bit of action! Laters, hippies!'

Aubrey and Ariadne watched her go, flinging herself up a tree and through the branches as if she were being chased by an imaginary goshawk.

There was a whistle above their heads.

'Hirundo!' cried Aubrey, spinning, as the swallow flew a graceful curve low above them. 'Oh, what a great day for flying!'

'It is, my mate, it is! Air's perfect, warm, light breeze, just right for record-breaking. Flies wherever you go, right Ariadne?'

'I know!' Ariadne replied. 'Choice of fatties this morning.' She paused and then she said quietly, half to herself, 'If only we could save some for the Great Hunger.'

Aubrey's hearing was very sharp and he heard her. He felt a spear of cold fear in his stomach. The Great Hunger, he thought,

with dread – just when everything seems
so beautiful! Then he remembered the
darkness between the lights of the pleiades,
the seven sisters, and how you cannot have
light without darkness. It's darkness, he
thought, which makes light so bright.

'Should we – start saving food?' he asked,
with dread. 'When's it coming?'

'Oh!' Ariadne exclaimed, 'no one knows;
maybe not long, maybe never. Don't worry
about it on a day like this! No one knows
the future.'

Aubrey thought about it. 'Do you think
I can help to stop it, Ariadne? I would do
anything – run away from school, travel
into the future – I'll do it. I'll do anything
to stop the Great Hunger from ... coming
anywhere near.'

'I'll ask Athene Noctua,' said Ariadne. 'But
you can't run away from school on the last
day of the holidays.'

'Ask her if I can help,' said Aubrey. 'I'll do
anything, I'll show her rambunctious!'

'So do you fancy it, Aubrey?' Hirundo called down. 'I know just where to get a Swallow Stone. And you can meet my mate – she's *only the most gorgeous bird in the whole world*! I'm supposed to be nest-building right now – you want to give me a hand?'

'I'd love to,' Aubrey said. 'I'm really tempted...'

'You,' said Ariadne, giving the palm

of his hand where she sat the slightest squeeze with her jaws, 'have got to do your homework. Take me back inside, please. Goodbye, Hirundo – happy nesting.'

'Next time eh, bru?' said Hirundo to Aubrey, and he dived suddenly, swooped up and whipped over the roof.

'Next time!' Hirundo called over his shoulder.

'Next time,' Aubrey whispered. 'Next time...!'

And carrying the enormous spider very carefully in his palm, the boy picked his way down the garden and headed back into the house.

AUBREY WILL RETURN TO FACE
THE GREAT HUNGER IN . . .

# AUBREY AND THE
# TERRIBLE SPIDERS!

# ACKNOWLEDGEMENTS

Dearest Rebeccabelle, Aubrey Buglet and Robin, Sally and John, Alexander and Logan and Meg, Jenny and Gerald, Chris and Jamie – Hi Jamie! – and Emma: dear family, thank you. (And special thanks, from all of us, to Jennifer Shooter, whose kindness, care and patience are endless.) Thank you Jane Matthews and Martha Brown, for your wonderful art and inspiration. Thank you Penny Thomas, Megan Farr, Janet Thomas, Claire Brisley and the Fireflies, for your tremendous work in bringing Yoots and Ladybirds to the world. Thank you, Peter Florence, Becky Shaw, Michael Morpurgo and Frank Cottrell Boyce for your terrific support. Thank you Jay Griffiths, Niall Griffiths, Debs Jones and Anna Gavalda, for your deep kindness. Thank you Zoë Waldie and Rosie Price, kind friends, and the perfect agent and assistant. And to the readers, teachers, librarians, parents and children especially, who have written to me about reading or listening to these stories: thank you!

## *Aubrey and the Terrible Yoot (Firefly, 2015)*

Aubrey is a rambunctious boy who tries to run before he can walk and has crashed two cars before he can drive one. But when his father, Jim, falls under an horrendous spell, Aubrey is determined to break it.

Everyone says his task is impossible but, with the help of the animals of Rushing Wood, Aubrey will never give up and never surrender, even if he must fight the unkillable spirit of despair itself: the Terrible Yoot...

Winner of the Branford Boase Award

Longlisted for the CILIP Carnegie Medal and the UKLA Children's Book Award

Winner of the North Somerset FCBG Children's Book Awards, quality fiction category.

Shortlisted for the Awesome Book Awards and the Surrey Libraries Children's Book Award

**Praise for Aubrey and the Terrible Yoot**

'Horatio Clare writes about animals as well as T. H. White.'

'...something very special - a book that is both pensive and
sparkling with originality and life. It is a testament to the
healing power of the imagination.'

'A beautiful and touching story, told in a unique and
refreshingly original style.'

' ... it shines a light on mental health without
ever feeling like a manual'
*Branford Boase judges*

'Here is writing and storytelling at its best. Here is a
wondrous tale, from a writer who loves language ...
a book of ideas, full of learning, though you might not know it,
because you are enjoying it so much. Here is a tale that sweeps
you along inside its magic, and its hope. At once bubbling with
joy, and at the same time dealing with the great sadness that
overcomes so many of us in our lives, the Terrible Yoot of the
title. A daring book, beautifully conceived, and supremely well
written. Horatio Clare has the voice of a great storyteller ...
a joy, a sheer joy!
*Michael Morpurgo*

'This is a completely wonderful insight into depression, I wish this book had been around to help someone I know. Poignant, funny, unique and ultimately uplifting, don't miss this gem.'
*Lara Mieduniecki, Blackwell's, Edinburgh*

'This remarkable novel is full of lyrical writing and sensible thinking...'
*Gwales.com*

'This is a special and unusual book ... some beautiful writing conjures up the sights, sounds and smells of the countryside with such clarity that you'll feel the damp ground beneath your feet, but it's also a moving and thoughtful description of a young boy trying to help his father through depression ... a story full of tenderness and understanding.'
*Lovereading4kids*

'Over the years I've met and read ... a host of great writers who can engage and transport children. Today I heard Horatio Clare introduce and launch *Aubrey and The Terrible Yoot*. It's about a rambunctious boy who needs to save his father. There was a small roomful of children who had their capacity for wonder and adventure met with humour and imagination and humanity of the most delightful kind. There was also the sense

that we were the first people to meet this book, and that that in
itself was a privilege and something we all might
get to tell our grandchildren about. We were there.'
*Peter Florence, director, Hay Festival*

'This clever book mixes myth, fable and modern
family life to create a vivid story that is not only full of magic
but also looks sympathetically at complex issues such as
depression. The story does not shy away from this difficult
topic, but describes it in a gentle and age-appropriate way,
engendering understanding rather than fear. This is an
enjoyable book that deals with important issues not often
covered in writing for this age range.'
*Books for Keeps Book of the Week*

' ...an imaginative and thoughtful adventure ...
the story is as lighthearted as it is serious.
Beautifully illustrated by Jane Matthews, both
young and old will enjoy this book.'
*We Love This Book*

'...an enjoyable, intriguing and important book.'
*Armadillo Magazine*